"You don't have any experience with men, do you?"

Read asked.

Marina couldn't resist reaching up to that wonderful mouth she ached to feel again. "I have what you taught me."

He swore under his breath. "That's not funny."

"It wasn't meant to be," Marina replied. "The only man who's ever held me like this is you. The only man to have ever kissed me as if he wanted to share the very air that fills my lungs is *you*."

"Stop it."

"You want me to lie?"

As if he was fighting his own will, he shifted one hand to cup her face. "I want you to quit sounding as if you think we can pick up where we left off."

Dear Reader,

Enjoy the bliss of this holiday season as six pairs of Silhouette Romance heroes and heroines discover the greatest miracle of all...true love.

Suzanne Carey warms our hearts once again with another **Fabulous Father:** *Father by Marriage*. Holly Yarborough thought her world was complete with a sweet stepdaughter until Jake McKenzie brightened their lives. But Jake was hiding something, and until Holly could convince him to trust in her love, her hope of a family with him would remain a dream.

The season comes alive in *The Merry Matchmakers* by Helen R. Myers. All Read Archer's children wanted for Christmas was a new mother. But Read didn't expect them to pick Marina Davidov, the woman who had broken his heart. Could Read give their love a second chance?

Moyra Tarling spins a tale of love renewed in *It Must Have Been the Mistletoe*. Long ago, Mitch Tyson turned Abby Roberts's world upside down. Now he was back—but could Abby risk a broken heart again and tell him the truth about her little boy?

Kate Thomas's latest work abounds with holiday cheer in *Jingle Bell Bride*. Sassy waitress Annie Patterson seemed the perfect stand-in for Matt Walker's sweet little girl. But Matt found his temporary wife's other charms even more beguiling!

And two fathers receive the greatest gift of all when they are reunited with the sons they never knew in Sally Carleen's *Cody's Christmas Wish* and *The Cowboy and the Christmas Tree* by DeAnna Talcott.

Happy Reading!

Anne Canadeo
Senior Editor

Please address questions and book requests to:
Silhouette Reader Service
U.S.: 3010 Walden Ave., P.O. Box 1325, Buffalo, NY 14269
Canadian: P.O. Box 609, Fort Erie, Ont. L2A 5X3

THE MERRY MATCHMAKERS

Helen R. Myers

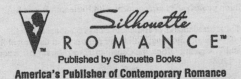

Silhouette
R O M A N C E™
Published by Silhouette Books
America's Publisher of Contemporary Romance

For Mrs. Ethel Jane Keyser
(Retired schoolteacher, Baltimore, Maryland)
With gratitude and love for the friendship, the many hand-stitched memories and for setting a graceful example of how to live life to the fullest.

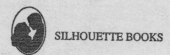 SILHOUETTE BOOKS

ISBN 0-373-19121-9

THE MERRY MATCHMAKERS

Copyright © 1995 by Helen R. Myers

This edition published by arrangement with Harlequin Books S.A.

® and TM are trademarks of Harlequin Books S.A., used under license. Trademarks indicated with ® are registered in the United States Patent and Trademark Office, the Canadian Trade Marks Office and in other countries.

Printed in U.S.A.

HELEN R. MYERS

satisfies her preference for a reclusive life-style by living deep in the Piney Woods of east Texas with her husband, Robert, and—because they were there first—the various species of four-legged and winged creatures that wander throughout their ranch. To write has been her lifelong dream, and to bring a slightly different flavor to each book is an ongoing ambition.

Admittedly restless, she sees that as a help to her writing, explaining, "It makes me reach for new territory and experiment with old boundaries." In 1993 the Romance Writers of America awarded *Navarrone* the prestigious RITA Award for Best Short Contemporary Novel of the Year.

We're moving to Marina'z houze!
me
Daddy
Ricky
my new mommy
by Molly Archer

Chapter One

"C'mon, Dad...don't say you're too tired. We did better on this week's video. And it's shorter!"

Read Archer sent his son a sidelong look, convinced he couldn't be that lucky. Sure he'd sat through last Saturday night's entire tape, but only because he'd been startled with Ricky and Molly's announcement that they'd come up with a way to help him find them a new mother.

At first he'd reasoned that if it stopped them from watching so much TV, and got them out into the fresh air a bit more, he could suffer through the results of their efforts. Maybe even get a laugh or two out of the thing. But that was before he'd realized they considered anything—correction, *anyone*—an improvement over the way things were now. He wasn't up to dealing with that emotional blow again. Not tonight when he was already bone tired, and feeling like the last guy on earth likely to be voted as single father of the year.

"You know, the more I think about it, the more doubtful I am about you two borrowing Billy's camera, kids. Are you sure Mr. and Mrs. Johnson know about that?"

"Yes, Dad. I told you last week."

There was a gentle rebuke in his eldest's voice, and as Read belatedly remembered the conversation, he cleared his throat. "Well, I'm telling you again. If you accidentally broke or lost it, I'd be obliged to buy a replacement, and I don't have that kind of money to throw away on luxuries for us, let alone for someone else."

His son scowled at him. "That's not it. You just don't want to meet anyone."

"'Cuz you can't 'ford no wimmen," Molly piped in, looking proud to be able to add to the conversation.

Read paused at scraping the stubborn remains of tuna and macaroni from the bottom of the casserole dish. His words sounded particularly crass coming out of his four-year-old's mouth. "I wish you'd listen that well when I tell you to eat your food while it's still warm, Missy."

Molly brushed aside a tangle of curls to eye the small mountain of mush that remained on her plate. "It's okay, Daddy. Warm don't make it taste no better."

Hell. What did you do when your kids were not only funny, but embarrassingly correct? After fourteen months of trying to be both father and mother to them, he may have learned how not to turn their underwear pink or blue in the wash, but his cooking still left much to be desired. But that didn't mean he wanted to think about getting involved in another relationship.

"Smarty-pants," he muttered, repressing most of his smile. "Then eat up so I can get these dishes done before midnight." Sunday was his one day to catch up on sleep, and he cherished that extra hour in bed.

"If she finishes, *then* will you watch the video?" Ricky asked, ever persistent. "Please, Dad?"

Read reached deep to try to make the boy understand. "Son...I thought we talked about this. Your mom was special and she would be hard to replace. Taking pictures of ladies around town isn't— First of all, they're strangers, and I told you last week that it wasn't polite to ask strangers personal questions like, 'Are you married?' and 'How old are you?'"

"We didn't this time, Daddy! We behaved really good."

"Is that so?" Read considered Molly's innocent face and wondered why he wasn't convinced. "What did you ask?"

"If they liked little girls." His daughter beamed and wriggled in her chair, clearly delighted with her inventiveness. "And every single one said yes!"

"Uh-uh!" Ricky adamantly shook his head. Like his sister, he had chestnut hair that gleamed with gold streaks under the fluorescent kitchen light, and although his was arrow straight, it was in bad need of a trim, just as his sister's was desperate for a brushing. "The last one didn't say anything of the kind!"

Molly pouted. "That's 'cuz you made her sad."

"Oh, great." Read looked from his four-year-old to his eight-and-a-half-year-old. "Who did you upset?"

"We don't know. But she was real pretty." Molly ignored her brother's dirty look. "She was my favorite 'cuz she looked like Snow White."

Ricky snorted. "She did not, dummy. Snow White didn't have hair anywhere near as long as that."

"Hey!" Read pointed the nylon scrubber at him. "No names. Besides, who just got a D on his last spelling test?"

"Yeah, big shot! And, anyway, she had black hair and white skin like Snow White, so there." After making a face at her brother, Molly sobered. "But you know what, Daddy? It was when she asked Ricky his name and he said Ricky Read Archer, that she got this funny look on her face. She asked if you were our daddy, and *that's* when she got sad."

Her brother groaned in frustration. "Don't you get it? She was sad because she *knew* Dad, but she didn't know about Mom going to heaven."

Read tried to match the description of the woman with his recollection of the various people he knew in the area, but without success. Of course, while Berryfield, Massachusetts, wasn't the smallest town west of Worcester, it was hardly a metropolis, either. The kids could have run into someone he'd done some custom work for awhile back.

"Did she happen to say where she lived?" he asked both of his offspring.

Although they signaled that she hadn't, Molly added, "She did say she'd been away for a long time."

Something inside Read tightened, while unwelcome images flashed before his eyes. He tried to ignore them—after all, he knew better than to think *she* would ever come back—but some devil's advocate in the most resolute part of his mind wouldn't leave him in peace. He heard himself ask, "Are you sure you didn't get the lady's name?"

"We didn't get a chance," Ricky told him. "She left right after that. You're not mad, are you? We didn't mean to say anything wrong."

"I know." Nevertheless, Read had to put down the dish he was holding because his hands were shaking.

"You sure don't look like you mean that."

On impulse he snatched up the towel on his shoulder and began drying his hands. "Let me have the tape, son."

Molly uttered a panicky sound. "Now? Wait a minute, Daddy! I'm not finished."

"I just need to see something," he replied, as she scooped up a spoonful of food and shoveled it into her little mouth. He touched her soft curls absently on his way to the living room. This couldn't wait. He had to make sure he was wrong about his hunch.

"Did you say the last one?" he asked his boy, as he put the cassette into the VCR machine.

Ricky handed him the remote control unit. "Yeah. It's about halfway through the tape."

Read fast-forwarded the tape and thought it nothing short of ironic that he stopped at the instant the kids focused on the woman. She'd paused to look into a store window, and when she turned and smiled into the camera, Read felt his heart skip a beat . . . then another . . . and another. Stunned, he lowered himself to the nearest seat—the coffee table.

Ten years. He hadn't seen her in an entire decade. Sometimes he went days, a week without thinking of her, or feeling the hollowness, the ache, her leaving had caused. Life had gone on. And yet he couldn't believe that she could be back, and he hadn't somehow known.

Don't do this, fool. You didn't want to know.

No, he hadn't. He'd worked hard to get on with his life, to build something good and solid for himself. He'd succeeded, too.

Then why's your pulse going nuts and your palms getting sweaty?

God, he felt like such a fraud. Just looking at her was a betrayal to Gwenn.

Those eyes... Slightly sloe-shaped and midnight dark, they seemed to look straight into his, immediately ensnaring him with a look that was as sad as it was startled. Those eyes were ancient in a face that remained incredibly youthful and lovely. She always had possessed a quality of gentleness and femininity, but that expression in her eyes told him that life hadn't left her unmarred. He didn't want to even begin thinking about what had happened. And yet another part of him wanted to reach through the television screen, to feel again her soft skin, and watch her eyes fill with emotion for him. For *him.*

"Damn."

"What is it, Dad? Is it true—you know her?"

He knew her. Read stopped the tape, and canned laughter from a popular but mindless sitcom filled the room. Oh, yes, he knew her.

"Dad?" Ricky frowned. "Why did you stop? You haven't even heard her talk yet."

That was the point. As it was, the memory of her voice filled his head and made the room, his past, feel as if it was all closing in on him, crushing him.

"Dad?"

He handed the buttons to his son and rose. "Watch whatever you want. I need to finish up in the kitchen."

It was an abrupt rejection, and he could sense his son's bewilderment and hurt; however, he couldn't do anything about that right now. Certainly not pretend. Before he could deal with anyone else's feelings, he needed time to get hold of his own.

Marina watched the middle-aged man return from his painstaking tour of the first floor of her house. "What do you think, Mr. Fields? Is my idea feasible?"

"Oh, yes, Miss Davidov." Every few steps he scribbled something else on his pad. "I think we could do an extremely satisfactory job for you as far as the structural changes are concerned. This is a wonderfully built old house. Terrific foundation, good solid walls... I don't foresee any difficulty in getting you the connecting effect from room to room you want on this floor. But when it comes to the specialty items... Well, let me be honest. I can get you bookcases, cabinets, shelving . . . you name it. But for a house of this quality I think you'd be doing yourself an injustice with settling for factory-made products.

"First of all there's the obvious look of mixing and matching. You want to stay with pieces that will fit the authenticity of the house's grand style. Outside, people see the brick and stonework, the century-old trees, the formal garden—why, this is one of the landmarks of Berryfield. Once people know they can come inside and they see the authentic hardwood floors, the sweeping staircase, all extraordinary detail work everywhere . . . Well, simply put, you don't want to destroy the effect with mass-produced items.''

Marina nodded, glad she'd called the building contractor. He'd been recommended to her by the agency that had been watching over the property. The man did seem to have a good feel for the house. "What do you suggest?"

"Custom work. A craftsman who'll respect the project he's taking on and provide an even tone with real wood—and I don't mean pine—to make proper display points for your merchandise.''

"You have someone in your firm who can do this?"

"No. To be honest, I can't afford someone like that full-time. Berryfield's economy is solid enough, thanks to being so close to a number of fine colleges, but these days people buy homes wanting built-in microwaves and extra bathrooms. A master carpenter's talents get wasted on installing prefab cabinetry and securing baseboards. But I can refer you to someone.''

"Very good."

"He would be glad for the work. He lost his wife not long ago, and between funeral expenses and raising two young children, things haven't been easy for them.''

Marina thought of the children she'd met downtown this morning. Her insides gave a strange little jolt.

Surely not . . . ?

But she found herself holding her breath as the contractor reached into his billfold and took out a business card, found herself amazed that her hands didn't shake as she accepted it and read the name. His name.

"Read Archer."

"That's right. You'll find he's quite the individualist, stubborn as hell about his work and sometimes a bit too proud for his own good. But a finer craftsman doesn't exist around here. I use him, myself, as often as I can."

Despite her jangling nerves, it pleased her to hear Read praised so highly. "I seem to remember the name somehow...."

"Could be. He's lived here all his life, and his folks used to operate a little general store near the high school you said you'd briefly attended. Maybe that's the connection. After he got out of the service, Read handled their deliveries until his folks got killed in an auto accident."

Poor Read! "I had no idea," she murmured, struggling to quickly come to terms with that revelation. The accident must have occurred shortly after her father had decided they should leave Berryfield. Once again she wished she'd been able to correspond with someone back here, but she knew the mail could never have kept up with them—or slipped past her father.

"It was sad," the contractor said, his expression grim. "Read sold the business and signed up for some woodworking classes at the college, thinking he'd learn some kind of trade. It turned out that he was a natural. His instructor found him an old guy in Worcester who was a magician with wood, and the rest is history. You give Read a call. He won't disappoint you."

That remained to be seen. But Marina thanked the man as she slipped the card into the pocket of her cardigan sweater, and for the remainder of the meeting, she listened to him go over figures and schedules.

"All right, Mr. Fields," she said, once he lifted his eyebrows to indicate the final decision was in her hands. "I'd like to open at least the front parlor to the public by early November, and more rooms by Thanksgiving, although I know there would still be noise and some traffic from your people. How soon can you start?"

"Well, a few weeks isn't much time, so we'd better get in here Monday morning. Will eight o'clock be good for you?"

"Perfect."

"Thank you, Miss Davidov, and welcome back to Berryfield," the man said warmly, shaking her hand. "I've often thought this was too fine a house to be standing empty, and I'm sure the business venture you're planning will be a big hit around here."

"Until Monday, Mr. Fields." But as she closed the front door after him, Marina's smile grew skeptical. She knew that—at least in the beginning—people would come strictly out of curiosity, to inspect Dmitri Davidov's daughter and the house where the eccentric Russian pianist-composer had worked while hiding from the world. Nothing more.

She reached into her pocket and drew out the business card the contractor had given her. This had to be a sign that what she'd done was right. Or was she trying to fool herself? Tomorrow she must find out, Sunday or not. She would contact Read then. She had no choice, since she had to be here for Mr. Fields's people on Monday.

"Tomorrow..." Would Read even speak to her? Only time would tell.

Read awoke to the sound of voices. Laughter and voices, he amended, wincing at a particularly loud squeal of giggles. *Jeesh...* His Molly could shatter beer mugs at two thousand paces.

He blindly reached for his alarm clock, then peered at it through the slit of his right eye. It was almost nine. He had to forgive the kids for getting restless. By now he should at least be out of the shower and on his way to mixing some pancake batter.

If he was lucky, they'd grown tired of waiting, maybe put some frozen waffles in the toaster or something. Then he remembered that they'd melted the insides of the toaster over a week ago and he hadn't yet had the chance to replace the small appliance.

"Up and at 'em," he muttered, kicking off an already tangled sheet and blanket.

Less than five minutes later he was dragging a crewneck sweater over yesterday's jeans and shuffling down the hallway. He wanted coffee and another nap, not necessarily in that order. But some interesting, if disconcerting, smells rising from below quickly canceled those ideas.

Dare he hope the kids had been watching some cooking channels for a change instead of cartoons?

Right, Archer. And you're going to get a Christmas present that doesn't have to get taped to the fridge.

"He inhales cholesterol," he heard Ricky declare from the kitchen. "Don't be stingy on the margarine for his pancakes or we'll have to pay."

"Pay? I don't think I understand," a soft, feminine voice replied.

"You know, *chores,* like walking the dog and cleaning the bird feeders." Molly made that sound like a life sentence on a chain gang. "Mommy loved birds and we have lots and lots of feeders, but none of us 'member to keep 'em filled."

"I see. It sounds as if you two work hard to earn your keep around here," the woman told them, sounding politely amused.

"You don't know the half of it," Ricky intoned.

But Read barely heard him. It was the woman his psyche had locked on to like some precision radar detector. That voice almost made him miss the last two steps on the stairs.

His knees were weak and his mouth bone-dry by the time he reached the kitchen doorway and saw the cozy picture of domesticity she made with his kids. It was her, all right; ten years or ten times ten, he would have recognized her anywhere.

Heaven help him.

It wasn't fair that she looked so good, even better than she'd appeared in the video. Dear God, he didn't need this.

"Hello, Read. It's good to see you. As you can see, I've intruded."

Yes, that was her way—to admit to everything, anything, leaving him with nothing to protest. All he could do was nod, circle her as if he suspected her of being a hallucination and back up to the coffeepot where a mug was already set out for him. That annoyed him, too. How was a man supposed to enjoy his anger when she'd thought of every courtesy and convenience?

He turned away from her to pour himself a full dose of the steaming brew. His hand shook. "Naturally," he muttered under his breath.

"Pardon?"

"When did you get back into town?" He tried to look casual as he returned to the entryway to use the doorjamb for support. It definitely made a sturdier spine than his, which at the moment felt ready to betray him.

"Tuesday, but I'm afraid I'll be unpacking for days to come." She glanced toward the table. "I hope you don't mind that I helped the children. They said they were starving."

"I'll bet they did." He eyed his two innocents. "And how did you two escape your chains and jimmy the basement door lock?" he said to them.

His son and daughter merely offered beatific smiles. It was Marina who exhibited unease. Bowing her head, she scooped the next batch of pancakes onto the platter that already held sausages and bacon.

"You're angry."

"Why should I be angry? I find it perfectly reasonable to have someone disappear out of my life. Vanish without a word of goodbye or go to hell, then wake up one Sunday ten years later and find her charming my kids in my own kitchen."

Molly clapped her hands with glee. "Daddy has to put a quarter in the oops jar," she sang, skipping to the pantry beside the refrigerator. She brought out an old mayonnaise jar and carefully set the half-full glass on the counter between him and Marina. "You said the H word, Daddy." She explained to Marina, "When he says a bad word, he has to put in a quarter, and when he fills it up, we get to have lunch anywhere we want."

Marina eyed the jar and then his daughter. Her lips twitched. "It looks as if you dine out frequently."

Molly nodded and grinned. "Uh-huh. 'Cuz the H and D words are his favorites. C'mon, Daddy. Pay up." She extended her tiny hand.

Read sipped his coffee and briefly reflected on how much simpler his world had been when he'd been single and his only responsibility was an aquarium occupied by a few dozen goldfish. Realizing that seemed a lifetime ago, he dug into his pocket and gave her the coin. "Now go wash your hands and sit down, Miss Mouth. You're about to eat."

"How do they like their eggs?" Marina asked him.

He found it incredible that her voice still bore a faint trace of the Russian accent that had intrigued him from the beginning. He would have thought she would have lost it by now. She was American by birth, having been born to parents who had defected from what had been the Soviet Union just in the nick of time for her arrival. But most of all it was her femininity that got to him, triggered memories of how it used to feel to hold her close to his heart and dream of the future he'd wanted to build for her, with her.

A sharp pain within his chest surprised him, and he stiffened against it. "No eggs. They'll do good to finish what you already have there."

"What about you?"

Did she think he could swallow anything while she was under his roof? "All I want is to know why you're doing this."

"The children asked me."

He lifted both eyebrows this time. "They phoned you and asked you to come over and make them breakfast?"

"I came over to talk to you. This...just happened."

Marina carried the platter to the table, already set by Ricky. The smile she gave him made his son stare as if she was presenting him with his own personal rainbow. Read understood the boy's reaction only too well; he'd felt poleaxed, too, the first time she smiled at him.

"What do we have to talk about?" he asked, feeling abruptly older and more than a little empty inside.

As the children attacked the food, she crossed over to him. She looked like a heroine from a Gothic novel in her black dress, which covered her from neck to wrist to matching suede boots. The palm-size silver cross dangling from a heavy chain to her narrow waist emphasized the dramatic bone structure of her heritage. But most dramatic was her wonderful hair; like onyx, it fell free nearly to her waist. It was a far different style to the braids wrapped tightly around her head that her father had preferred she wear.

"Read...my father passed away last month." She stopped no more than a yard from him. "Perhaps the news was carried locally on TV?"

"I wouldn't know." Unlike his children, he rarely had the time or interest in watching television. And he didn't plan on offering any condolences, either. Dmitri Davidov had hated his guts, and by the time the world-renowned pianist and composer had left Berryfield, taking his daughter with him, Read had reciprocated those feelings. In spades.

By her expression, it was clear Marina wasn't about to question his quick denial. "He caught a cold in Budapest," she told him instead. "We took a train to Paris, and by the time we arrived, his condition had deteriorated. Pneumonia set in. I still can't believe he's gone."

She gripped the Russian Orthodox cross and looked away for a moment. Even so, Read could see her fight back tears, and had to lower his gaze to his coffee to keep from weakening and doing something stupid.

"So you're here to sell the house." That was a good thing. Let it change hands. It had stood long enough as an embarrassing testament to his youth and naïveté.

"Sell? Why, no."

"No?"

"I told you, I've moved back to Berryfield."

She'd mentioned unpacking. That didn't necessarily mean she was staying permanently.

After delicately wiping at the corners of her eyes, she wrapped her arms around her waist and managed a proud smile. "I'm going to be a businesswoman."

He was so bowled over by the revelation about her intention to stay on, the rest was slow to register. "What kind of— Doing what?"

"Marina's going to turn her house into a Christmas store, Daddy!"

Read had just enough composure left to shoot his daughter a look of mild rebuke. "It's Miss Davidov to you, young lady, and this is grown-up talk. You keep your nose in that plate."

"Yeah, like an anteater," Ricky said, chortling.

"Daddy!" Molly pointed at her brother.

"That's enough—both of you." Read gestured their guest toward the hallway. "Would you mind?" Without waiting for her to respond, he led the way.

In the entry hall, he discreetly kicked one of Ricky's dirty socks as close to the steps as possible and ran a hand over his hair. "What are they talking about?"

"A shop based solely on Christmas items, doesn't that sound fun? The idea came to me several times over the years. You see, we traveled a great deal, and while my father was in a practice session or in meetings, I had hours of free time on my hands. You can only tour museums so often and for so long. At least that's how it was for me," she said with a self-deprecating grimace. "So I explored the specialty shops next. They were an escape for me—a fantasy world, especially around the holidays. Then it came to me that there might be others like me, people who, for one reason or another, might have missed out on such delights. Do you think I'm right?"

"Beats me."

Marina's hopeful expression waned. But after a few seconds she continued determinedly. "In any case, over the past month I've been talking to artisans and craftsmen, and I've purchased a modest inventory to stock at least one room in the house. Enough to open right after Halloween."

She lifted her chin. Read thought the subtle movement gave her a regal air that a Bolshoi ballerina would have envied. "And?" he demanded, increasingly uncomfortable because he sensed there was more. Much more.

"In the meantime I've hired a contractor to make some structural alterations."

Read couldn't believe what he was hearing. She did sound serious. "What kind of alterations?"

"Connecting the rooms...closing off the kitchen...creating an office area behind the checkout counter. That sort of thing. I plan to turn the entire first floor into a store, Read."

It didn't make sense, but he was beginning to feel hunted, and that made him angry. His memories were tough enough to cope with. Did she have to move back and rub salt in those old wounds?

"Don't tell me your daddy didn't leave you with enough money to live in the fashion to which you'd grown accustomed?" he muttered, more unhappy than ever that she'd returned.

It came as no surprise to see her blanch, even draw back. She might be American by birth, but she certainly wasn't liberated. An American woman might even have taken a swing at him, but all Marina did was study him with those haunting eyes and clench her hands more tightly. "You're more bitter than I anticipated. I thought...I'd told myself that if I could come here and explain—"

"The time for explanations was ten years ago. You didn't bother. You just left."

"But I had no choice."

"Didn't you?" Realizing how intense he sounded, he forced himself to relax, even shrug. "In any case it no longer matters. The question is what do you want from me?"

For an instant she looked as if she might not tell him, might snatch up her wrap from the chair behind her and race out the front door. Then she moistened her lips and said, "Your professional services. Mr. Fields recommended you to me. For the shelving and various display furnishings. He said you were the best craftsman he knew. Someone who would understand and enhance the architecture." She waved her hand in a way that denoted confusion, helplessness. "I had no idea of your profession, Read. This is all a coincidence."

"And that little performance with my kids yesterday was a coincidence, too?"

"Performance?" She sighed. "Read. You once said I would have to wear a burlap sack over my head to win a hand of poker. Do you think I've changed that much?"

He *thought* he should never have gotten out of bed. He thought he was a fool to have listened to her for as long as he already had. Aware only that he wanted this fiasco to be over, he shook his head. "It's no good."

"But, Read—"

"I can't help you, all right?"

She tilted her head and eyed him sadly. "Can't or won't?"

He forced the words out before he lost his conviction. "It doesn't matter. What does is that you don't belong here."

Chapter Two

Marina didn't quite succeed in repressing a shiver, but then she'd never been treated to such bitter rejection before, either. Even when the Soviet Union had ceased to exist and her father had agreed to return to his homeland to do a series of concerts, they both had been treated with the utmost respect and affection, not any of the cool disdain and suspicion they'd feared. That it should be Read who exposed her to the worse side of human behavior was unbearable.

Afraid he might see how badly he'd hurt her, she spun around, snatched up her cape and rushed out of the house. It was a miracle that she didn't topple down the steps in her haste to get away, and she made it nearly a half block before she grew aware of the nip in the early October air. Only then did she pause long enough to slip her cape over her shoulders.

For the first time since stepping back on American soil, she wished she owned a car. Her father had never seen the need to have one, nor had he ever obtained a license himself. While living here in town, they'd relied on the elderly couple who'd cared for the house and property if they'd needed transportation. And she didn't need a car because Berryfield wasn't so large as to be inaccessible by foot. Her house was only a few blocks away. But thanks to Read's behavior, she suddenly felt as if there were eyes peering out at her from behind every curtained and shaded window. Dear heaven, the last thing she wanted to do was become as paranoid as her father about being watched.

Still, she was on her own now, and the Pedersons were long gone. A management company had been in charge of keeping the house in good order, and she'd just ended that arrangement. She needed to do something about getting a driver's license and a vehicle as soon as possible. She never wanted to endure this kind of embarrassment again.

Oh, Read. How could he have said what he did? She couldn't believe it. She had hoped, in spite of the unorthodox way they'd parted ten years ago, that he'd somehow understood what had happened. That they—

Well, there was no sense in dwelling on what had been now. Clearly, she'd lost more than her father. She'd lost the only real friend she'd ever had, too. Read had left no doubt that not only didn't he want to help her with the house, he didn't want any contact with her at all.

When she reached her house, she quickly unlocked the front door, bolted it behind herself, reset the se-

curity system and slumped against the heavy door.
Gone was the excitement and anticipation she'd felt
earlier. Suddenly, she was exhausted and so alone. The
huge house was utterly void of the joy and laughter
she'd experienced while around Read's children.

She could almost hear her father's rich baritone
chiding her, "But this is who we are, Marina. Why do
you fight it and me? Wasn't I was right about *him?*
He's not for you."

"*Ochin' zhahl',* Papa. I'm so sorry."

So many hopes shattered. So many dreams turned
to ash. What was she going to do?

By Monday morning she was still wondering.

Not surprisingly, it had been difficult getting
through the rest of the weekend, although she enjoyed being back in the house. She might not want
such silence and solitude to represent her life now, but
she was used to being alone. She'd grown up under-
standing her father's need for having absolute silence
while he practiced and composed. Even Mrs. Pederson had been forced to work under the sternest re-
strictions, because her father hadn't tolerated strangers
"lurking and snooping about and making a racket."
As a result, Marina had often done much of the
housework herself.

Her homecoming had changed nothing in that respect. While the management company had hired
someone to prepare the house for her return, the
woman had been restricted to only certain rooms. As
a result, Marina had much work ahead of her. It was
also no surprise that despite all the physical labor, her

mind focused on her troubles, and the disappointment and worrying took their toll.

Throughout the night she tossed and turned, struggling through disturbing dreams and more than one nightmare. By five o'clock Monday morning she threw back the part of the down comforter and sheet that hadn't already slid to the floor and took a long, rejuvenating shower. Afterward she dabbed on the foundation she used on only special occasions to hide the shadows under her eyes, a little blush, a brighter lipstick than usual and headed downstairs. She felt nowhere near terrific, but she had come to a decision.

She was determined not to let Read's anger control her for another moment. She also knew she couldn't let him change her plans for the future.

Her clothes helped give her a bit of a lift. She'd dressed in one of her new pants outfits, a deep chocolate brown with the tunic sweater boldly accented in black and gold. Pants had been forbidden by her father; he'd seen them as unseemly attire for a proper young lady. But she liked the way the slim slacks emphasized the length of her legs, and the hint of gold thread in the sweater added a touch of luster to pale skin she thought needed more help than usual this morning.

She finished securing her hair over her right shoulder with a black velvet ribbon just as she arrived in the kitchen. After flipping on all three light switches, she turned on the new portable radio she'd placed by the wall telephone. It was set to an easy-listening station. Not exactly pop rock by any stretch of the imagination, which won a crooked smile from her, but some changes took longer than others. Besides, she needed to be able to hear herself think.

Once she put on some water to boil for *cháhy*—or tea, as she was trying to start thinking of it, now that she didn't have to talk, write and think in her father's native tongue—she opened the leather-bound notebook she'd left on the counter last night. On the top page of the tablet she considered the drawing she'd sketched of the house—the way she hoped it would appear by Christmas. It wasn't a professional job by any means; she'd never had any training in art. But she was rather pleased with the winter-wonderland effect she'd achieved by inking in all the garland and ribbon bows she planned to drape along the waist-high stone wall that fenced in the three-acre property. That and the lights to be strung over dozens and dozens of the shrubs and evergreens would provide a fairy-tale quality to the estate, which possessed a surreal quality, anyway.

She imagined how children would soon press their noses against car windows as their parents drove them past the house, the same way she used to gaze longingly at decorated houses when she was a child. Although hardly cruel, her father hadn't believed in that aspect of the holiday; he'd seen that as "offensively commercial," and preferred a more spiritual approach to the holidays.

But this wonderful house all but cried out for more. It wouldn't for long, though, not if she had anything to say about things. And she did. That was the wonder of it. Despite the deep sadness she felt for the loss of her father, there was an undeniable sense of excitement and freedom, too.

The boiling water got her attention. She poured it into the fine china cup and saucer she'd set out on the counter last night, and let the tea steep, thoughtfully eyeing the next page, where she'd drawn the inside floor plans. If only Read had given her a chance to show him these. But he hadn't been in the mood to think about anyone else but himself, and she couldn't blame him for that. When she left ten years ago, she'd hurt him terribly.

Theirs had been an unexpected, wondrous romance that ended before it really had a chance to fully blossom. She'd been fresh out of high school, a private, restricted one. Read had just finished four years in the air force and was helping his parents at their small grocery store. They met when bad weather brought him with a delivery to the house.

He'd arrived in dripping-wet leather and denim, a breathtaking example of American masculinity, leaving her as dumbstruck as if she'd never been alone with a man in her life—which she hadn't. Her strict and protected upbringing hadn't prepared Marina for someone so physical and direct as Read.

No, her heart never stood a chance. He swept her off her feet with the kind of bold romance she'd only glimpsed when sneaking a few minutes of television, or one of the cherished novels that were so difficult to keep from her father. Within weeks she'd found herself wildly in love with a man five years her senior age-wise, and a lifetime older in experience. Small wonder that when her father discovered what had been going on behind his back, he accepted the first offer to travel that came along. Thereafter, he kept a grueling pace until his death last month.

Ten years of globe-trotting . . . and Read couldn't know how she'd been helpless to do anything about it. Well, not at first. Not when it mattered.

But Read hadn't suffered long, had he? Marina removed the tea bag from her cup, added a cube of sugar and stirred thoughtfully. Ricky told her he would be nine soon, and that delightful imp, Molly, was four. The reality of them meant Read had met someone and married her not long after *she* left Berryfield; so what right did he have to treat her as if she'd ruined his life? At least he had two adorable children to love. She had no one.

With or without his help, somehow she would go on. She wasn't a child any longer, but twenty-eight, an independent woman, both emotionally and financially. If she didn't make her own happiness, she had no one to blame but herself.

She was repeating that warning a few hours later when she heard the buzzer that announced Mr. Fields and his crew had arrived at the front gates. Drawing a deep breath, she pressed the button that let them enter and prepared herself to take the first step in achieving at least a few of her goals.

"I thought I would stay with the boys this first day," Mr. Fields said, after shaking her hand. "Thereafter, I'll be in and out, but I'll put my best foreman in charge, who just happens to be my son. However, if at any time you have a question he can't answer, or a complaint, don't you hesitate to call me."

Marina liked the middle-aged man's earnestness, just as she'd liked his honest face the other day when they first talked. After letting him introduce her to the crew, she drew him aside to tell him of her bad news.

"Mr. Archer turned me down, Mr. Fields."

"You're kidding!"

"I wish I was."

Phil Fields pushed his baseball cap off his forehead. "But this project is perfect for him—and he's always been eager for more business."

"Well, apparently not as much as you thought." Definitely not her business.

"Let me call him. There must be some misunderstanding."

As he started for the kitchen phone, Marina touched his arm. "Wait. I haven't told you— You should know something first." She took a deep breath to compose herself, and gather her courage. Embarrassing as it would be, she had to tell him. It wouldn't be fair to put Read on the spot, regardless of how disappointed she was with his behavior. "It turns out that we know each other," she blurted out. Belatedly, she realized that suggested more than she wanted to share. "Knew each other."

As expected, the contractor eyed her owlishly from behind his thick glasses. "No kidding?"

"When you first mentioned his name, I recognized it, of course. But I had no idea he'd gone into carpentry and— Oh, dear, this is embarrassing."

"Now, now." Mr. Fields patted her hand. "Surely there's nothing to be embarrassed about. After all, you were quite young when you left here."

"True. But... all I can say, Mr. Fields, is that our reunion wasn't what you would call pleasant."

The man thrust out his barrel-like chest. "Was he rude to you? If he was, I'll straighten him out, you can put money on that."

"Please, no. He's made his decision and I have to honor it."

"But if he won't do the job—"

"Then you'll have to recommend someone else."

Phil Fields spread his arms wide. "There isn't anyone else. Not anyone who doesn't have to drive from way out of town, which in bad weather means not showing up at all, which then delays progress and might affect your ability to open on schedule." He scratched at his encroaching bald spot. "I always anticipate problems, but I can't say I expected anything like this."

"Surely something else can be arranged?"

He shot her a droll look. "You can go away for six months, while I bring in slower, possibly less-talented people. Sure, the situation's not impossible. But is that the desirable solution? That's something only you can decide."

True. And it was a decision Marina had no problem making. "Mr. Fields, do you have any idea what it's like to live out of a suitcase, week after week, month after month? To have no permanent home, nowhere you feel absolutely comfortable and relaxed? Always having to rely on someone to deliver food to you, clean clothes, clean sheets for the bed? Never knowing your neighbors, let alone establishing long-term friendships?"

The contractor tugged at his ear and wrinkled his nose. "Well, if you had my neighbors, that wouldn't sound half-bad." But after the gentle teasing, he quickly added, "I know what you're driving at, Ms. Davidov. I'm just not sure I can guarantee you a best-of-all-worlds scenario."

"Understood, Mr. Fields, but I'm not leaving my home again. One room. I can establish The Christmas House with just one room. Look." She picked up the notebook that was never too far out of her reach these days. "If necessary, I can take some furniture from the study and elsewhere to use as display tables. But if your men could make me some kind of shelving, that would be a wonderful start."

The contractor grimaced. "Ms. Davidov, if we were talking about any other room, maybe we could work something out. But not that one. The first impression people get upon entering this house should be one of class and distinction, and it's a bright room. You can't have anything but the best, and none of my men could create work to compare with your furnishings."

His impassioned speech made Marina smile. "Your sensitivity to the house and my father's reputation as a perfectionist is touching, Mr. Fields. But you should know that he often had to settle for less than perfect behind the scenes to achieve a goal before an audience. Out-of-tune pianos in practice halls, borrowed clothes because luggage had been lost, performances in buildings with horrible lighting and even worse acoustics... This would be just another of those hurdles, as far as I'm concerned."

But Phil Fields clearly would have none of that. "That's a generous attitude, Ms. Davidov. Only it's not going to make you like those shelves any better if my guys do them."

"Then don't do them," came a baritone pronouncement from the doorway.

* * *

Read watched Marina's reaction. He had to admit he enjoyed the shock and confusion in her eyes, even if he didn't quite trust the innocence all that seemed to enhance.

"I thought you turned the lady down," Phil Fields said, recovering enough to draw himself to his full height and glare up at him.

Having worked with the older man for several years, Read knew when to disregard a businessman's blustering. "Maybe I changed my mind."

While the contractor considered that, he noted the surprise and pleasure that played across Marina's face. She looked lovely this morning, and whether he wanted her to or not, she spawned a deep-seated hunger in him that he hadn't felt in a long time.

"Are you saying you've reconsidered?" his sometime business associate demanded.

He didn't bother taking his gaze off Marina. "I think that's something between Ms. Davidov and myself. Can we talk?" he added directly to her.

She managed a nod, then murmured something soothing to Phil that he couldn't hear. Although the elderly man didn't look happy about being left out, he deferentially stepped back to let her lead Read from the room. Read followed, drinking in the sight of her lithe figure, her glorious hair, her feminine walk. He became so preoccupied, he didn't realize where she was taking him until they reached the regal study that he guessed had been her father's hermitage.

"Nothing like rubbing it in," he muttered under his breath.

The room was a designer's dream, fit for a prince—tapestry-covered walls, the finest woodwork, yards of bookcases and furnishings that belonged in a museum. But it wasn't exactly a study, for in the place of a stately desk stood the grand piano. Elegant though it was, Read hated it on sight, because it represented what he had lost when Marina left him. All the more reason to resent her for bringing him here.

"This may not be the room to have this discussion," he said, feeling a new rigidness in his body as she closed the solid French doors behind them.

"It's the most soundproof in the house."

Did she think he'd come here to cause a scene? Hardly, although in all honesty he'd come without having decided what he did hope to achieve. As his gaze once again drifted over her, he decided some of the possibilities were better left in the furthermost recesses of his mind. Shrugging at her comment, he began wandering around the room.

He paused by a side table to admire the wood carving of a bear, then moved on to a hand-painted commode and around the piano to consider the view of the grounds. But he couldn't relax. Dmitri Davidov remained too much of a presence here.

"Will you keep that?" he asked abruptly, turning to nod at the piano. To him it would always resemble a great black predator.

"Yes. For now." Marina approached the highly polished instrument, but did not touch it. "Someday I may donate it to a conservatory, or perhaps a museum. Several have mentioned they would like to have it."

"You don't want to play it yourself?"

"I can't play."

That revelation stunned him. "Can't?"

"No. Besides being a perfectionist, my father was wholly competitive. He could never have dealt with the possibility that I could have a natural talent—or worse, had no talent at all."

"That's . . . twisted."

"That's focus."

Absolutely no emotion showed on her face, leaving her as visually perfect but remote as a mannequin. Read didn't like the effect at all. "How can you defend him?"

"I'm not. I'm explaining who he was. His weren't necessarily admirable traits, especially not to people who have never experienced such passion. But without them, I'm not sure art would exist in the form we've come to know it." Her look held challenge. "You're reported to be a painstaking craftsman. Surely you know what it's like to be fixated to the point of obsession."

Did she really want an answer to that? Read doubted it. Rather than respond, he eyed the piano with new loathing. "If I were you, I'd get a chain saw and turn the damned thing into a lawn chair."

That won a brief laugh from her. "The thought did cross my mind . . . when I was thirteen. But he chose that weekend to compose an adagio for me. It was a strange experience to hear something so exquisite played on something I resented so. In a matter of moments his piano became a friend rather than an enemy to me. A few years later I heard Candice Bergen reminisce about her father and the odd relationship she'd shared with him and his puppet, Charlie Mc-

Carthy. I realized there were other people who could parallel in a way what my life was like.''

It was an interesting admission, and Read knew it was just the tip of the iceberg regarding her complicated relationship with her father and his work. But he knew he couldn't listen to too much more without having to deal with the danger of caring again. He thought of a safe question. ''Will you let the public in here?''

''Not as I would the other rooms, no.''

''That might be best. If you make this one of the display rooms, you'll have heck trying to keep the kids from hammering out 'Chopsticks' on it. Wouldn't that have the old man rolling over in his grave?''

''It can be locked. I did think of turning it into a small museum,'' Marina said, eyeing the room thoughtfully. ''Maybe setting out some photos, his awards . . . that sort of thing.''

''Berryfield's answer to the Smithsonian?''

Marina's disappointment in his sarcasm was palpable across the few yards that separated them. ''I don't blame you for being bitter.''

''Is that supposed to make me feel better or kinder toward your father?''

''No. But you should restrict your anger to me, and not blame my heritage.''

''That's all right. I have plenty of animosity to go around.''

Her wince was fleeting, but poignant. ''Read. I'd hoped I hadn't hurt you too deeply. I survived those first weeks by convincing myself that I'd overestimated how you felt about me.''

"Maybe I should have tried that technique. You look as if the process agreed with you."

But that wasn't true, either. She looked about as substantial as a puff of smoke. On top of that, if she'd slept more than a few hours since he'd all but bitten her head off yesterday, no one would be more surprised than him.

Ashamed, Read turned away to stare outside at the evergreen garden that looked straight out of *Alice in Wonderland*. "Why did you come back?" he demanded, for the second time in so many days, but this time without his previous resentment.

"This is my house now. The only home I've ever really had."

"It's a piece of property...one you turned your back on for almost a decade."

"But I never forgot it," she replied, a slight tremor in her voice. "Never. If you believe otherwise, then you know me less than I thought. I may have spent most of my life living out of a suitcase, but I always hoped to return here."

"Why not sell the place and start over somewhere else?"

"Would you prefer me to do that?"

"It doesn't matter what I think." He knew he sounded like a petulant five-year-old and silently swore at himself for the weakness...and his lack of honesty.

Even so, she caught on to him. "Suppose you tell me why you are here, Read?"

"Beats me."

"Just passing by, is that it?"

His grunt was more of a growl. "I wanted you to know that you ruined what was left of my weekend."

"So you thought you'd come by and ruin my week."

Her calm, quiet observation held just enough mockery to finish making him feel like a heel. Needing her to understand, he did an about-face. "My kids aren't speaking to me. They think I chased you off."

"You did."

"But you know why."

She shook her head, her expression sympathetic. "That was a decade ago, Read. Ancient history. I'm not expecting anything from you on a personal level."

"Aren't you?"

He watched her lift her clasped hands to her lips. With her clear dark eyes and black hair, she reminded him of a young Madonna. But Marina Davidov wasn't that innocent. He'd been stung deeply once for making that mistake, but never again.

"Oh, Read," Marina said, as if his renewed resolve was written on his face. "You think I knew what my father was planning?"

"Yes. You had to. You couldn't have disappeared so quickly without being aware that something was up."

Her laugh was brief and more than a little hard. "Oh, really? Let me give you a crash course in Russian culture. Secrecy is ingrained, Read. The people are extremely insecure, and they find it difficult, if not distasteful, to admit to an error. So they go through life playing everything very close to the chest. On top of that they're extremely superstitious—another reason not to verbalize too much before acting.

"The night my father and mother defected from the Soviet Union, for example," she said, looking as if she'd experienced the event herself, "they'd been in Moscow for a concert honoring the new ambassador from the United States. My father didn't even tell my mother that he'd decided they were to leave the Soviet Union until that morning. In a matter of hours after his performance, they were under U.S. diplomatic protection and being rushed to the West."

Read felt a pang of sympathy for Davidov's wife, who, he knew from previous talks with Marina, had been pregnant with their only child at the time. What kind of man did that to a woman he was supposed to love and trust above anyone else?

"Are you saying when you left it was all his idea, too?" he asked Marina with a frown.

"When I told him about you.. about us, he barely said a word. Two nights later, when I was supposed to meet you for your friend's Christmas party, he informed me that he'd accepted an invitation to play in England and that we were to leave immediately. He'd actually packed for me while I was at the library."

His heart pounded with remembered fury and hurt. Read clenched the hands he'd thrust into his jacket pockets. "You couldn't take a second to call and tell me?"

"He'd already removed the phones."

"What about sending me a note or letter?"

"I tried. He found them."

She said it so calmly, without apology or accusation, as if announcing a sheet of cookies had been burned in a too-hot oven and needed to be thrown out. It made what she said all the more impossible for Read to deal with. Where was this Russian passion he'd heard so much about? Where was *her* fury and grief?

As if picking up on his thoughts, Marina shook her head. "You have a son going on nine years old, Read. Exactly how long did *you* brood over my abrupt departure?"

She had him there. He lowered his gaze to the expensive-looking rug between them. "Things...happened."

"They always do."

"Look," he muttered, needing no help in beating himself up for what he did. "Gwenn was a nice girl. And she deserved better than what she got from me, but I tried to make her happy."

To his surprise Marina looked sympathetic. "I hope you loved her."

"I learned to. Later."

"How did she die?"

"She'd had a stroke during her labor with Molly. She had another fourteen months ago. This time she didn't pull through."

Marina wrapped her arms around her waist. "How sad for the children."

"But not for me, eh?"

"It's obvious you won't accept my sympathy or anything else if I offered it, Read. But even I can see your children need more attention than they're getting."

"I'm not neglecting my kids."

"I didn't say you were."

"Just keeping a roof over our heads and them clothed is a full-time job."

"Undoubtedly." She eyed him for another long moment. "And that's why you're here, is that it?"

He exhaled, glad to have that behind him. "I can't afford to continue letting my personal feelings interfere with what I know is best for Ricky and Molly."

"At least you're big enough to put their welfare ahead of your personal feelings."

"I always have—and will."

Twin spots of color spread in Marina's cheeks. "Read, I don't want to make this a painful experience. I'd hoped after I had a chance to explain about the past that you and I could be...well, at least cordial to one another."

Cordial? Did people actually speak that way in the circles she traveled in? If so, it was just another reminder of how wrong they'd been for each other, mismatched from the beginning. Her father had done them both a favor. So why did he still feel such anger?

"I don't know if that will be possible," he replied, owing her the truth.

Marina bowed her head. "I see. Would you be happier if we communicated through Mr. Fields?"

He could imagine what the rest of the men working for the contractor would say to that, not to mention Fields himself. "It wouldn't work. No, if we do this—and I do mean *if*—we'd have to learn to deal with each other directly."

"I would like us to try." When she lifted her gaze to his, that truth shimmered in her thick-lashed eyes. "Mr. Fields does say you're the man for the job."

Aware he was becoming mesmerized, he had to swallow to find his voice. "Then I suppose you'd better show me around and tell me what you had in mind, and I'll...I'll let you know if that's feasible or not."

Chapter Three

Where to start? Despite his agreement to at least listen to her plan, Marina was intimidated by Read's unmistakably resentful attitude. She hadn't expected this to be easy—no, that wasn't true, either. In her dreams she'd imagined quite a different reunion for them. But she'd thought she was prepared to at least sell her idea to him, if not herself. Win him over business-wise. The realization that he would be looking at everything from a dubious, and worse, critical standpoint had her doubting her ability to achieve even the slightest point with him.

"I should start by telling you why I want to create The Christmas House," she began, leading the way into the large circular foyer.

"You already did. During your travels, you spent your time in shops to alleviate your boredom," he replied, his tone indifferent. "You think a college-orientated town like Berryfield will have enough frustrated housewives who share that kind of feminine malaise.''

So, he wasn't through wanting to punish her. Marina clasped her hands more tightly and faced him again. "Not quite. I want to do this because we never celebrated holidays. Do you understand what that's like for a child? To grow up without the magic of knowing your birthday is special? To make excuses to classmates for not participating in seasonal celebrations? There is a joy in giving, but it was a late discovery for me. There is a grace in learning to receive, but I'm still trying to discover it.''

Although the muscles along his jaw worked, Read's expression remained stony. "Why didn't you? Your father didn't ascribe to any Iron Curtain political dogma, did he?''

"I told you, he believed in his music. Anything that detracted from it was either discouraged or simply rejected.''

Read's look held doubt. "You're serious? No Christmas trees or Easter Bunny?''

It hurt that he'd forgotten, because she had explained it to him once. Back then. "No dressing up for Halloween or exchanging Valentine cards with friends. No Thanksgiving dinner to celebrate the country that had given us sanctuary and a standard of living that would never have been possible in the old country.'' She winced inwardly at that expression. It was one of her father's, and underscored how ingrained his influence remained in her life.

Read was silent for several long seconds. "I knew he'd been strict, but what you're describing is closer to imprisonment."

"Words and definitions." Marina shrugged, avoiding his direct but troubled blue-gray eyes. "He was my father. That was my life and it wasn't conventional. What does it matter now? It's today I care about. This house—" she spread her arms as if it was possible to embrace the place "—understands. Like me, it's been locked up and empty for too long. It's endured too much silence despite all the music, and many more temper tantrums. It wants and deserves to hear children . . . laughter. It yearns for *life.*"

Read stared, his look cautious, dubious. "I'm not sure I understand all that."

"Of course you don't," she replied, almost sympathetic. "You were born with freedom. People who are can't conceptualize what it's like to live without it or understand how precious it is. But I do . . . and a good part of why I'm doing this with the house is to give myself the childhood I missed. I know I must do that if I'm to get on with my life."

"It sounds as if you have a lot of territory to cover," Read said, his voice not unkind.

She smiled at that verbal olive branch. "I know. Come look." She continued to where she'd placed her folder and showed him the handful of brochures, photographs and notes. "This is just the first group of artisans I'll be dealing with. I want you to see these, the kind of things I'll be displaying, so that when you tour the house, you can tell me if what I'm asking for makes sense, or if there's a better way to display the items."

"I'm not sure I would be any good."

Marina decided to ignore that. "This is the angel tree," she said, opening to the photograph of the huge Norfolk pine filled with every kind of crystal, porcelain and wooden angel imaginable. "I'm not sure what kind of tree I'll use, but I thought I'd set it here in the middle of the foyer on this round table, so that people see it almost as soon as they enter the house. Then I wanted the walls lined with display tables and armoirs that I can fill with the items that are on the tree."

Read looked from the picture to the old English table and its distance to the walls. "Isn't that too far away? The idea of displaying stock is fine, but maybe of other items. If this was something I was planning, I'd put the decorations on the tree beneath this table. Use some kind of heavy cover to protect this table first. Maybe taffeta in gold, or a plaid, and then circle the floor with large copper and brass buckets around the table to hold your inventory. Or baskets, something like that. It'll keep people from getting too close to the tree and the table and accidentally knocking anything down."

"I like that." Encouraged, Marina showed him the parlor and the sketch she'd made of how she wanted it to appear after Mr. Fields's people cut the doorway from the parlor to the formal dining room. "I've asked for the parlor to be done first. This will have another display table in the center, and whatever else you can think of to show off the bulk of what I'll have to offer this year. Of course, if you think there's time to do more . . . ?"

"Exactly how long do you think it takes to make a piece of furniture?"

Marina touched his arm. "I didn't mean to offend you, Read."

His gaze fell to where she had her hand, and he eased away from her. "Never mind."

"No, really. I didn't mean to sound as if I thought it was something you could do like a paint-by-number picture. That's why I asked for someone with your talent to help me." Despite the knot in her stomach at his reaction to her, she forced herself to go on. "Why don't you tell me what's feasible?"

He bowed his head. His hair, shades fairer than his children's, caught the chandelier light bringing out flashes of gold. Its thickness and health made Marina yearn to touch it again as she used to during those stolen moments when he held her close to his heart.

"Well, maybe I can do something." He gestured toward the parlor. "Let me actually walk through the rooms."

Taking hope from that, Marina led him to the large coat closet she wanted transformed into a checkout area. Then they went to the formal living room, where sheets still covered the furniture, but the French influence was unmistakable.

"I wanted to rearrange this room, get rid of several pieces that I could use elsewhere and put up several trees. I'm calling this the Ornament Room. Except for the angel tree, most of the ornaments I'll carry will be stocked here. Later the parlor will be for my most collectible, one-of-a-kind items."

"Are the couch and chairs among the items going?"

"No. I want to leave them to make the room look like a real living room."

Read lifted eyebrows much darker than his hair. "About two weeks of three-foot-tall urchins traipsing through the place, and it should look plenty real."

She'd thought about that, but she planned to have attendants in each room eventually and hoped to keep damage under control. As she explained that to him, she drew out the drawing she'd sketched of the final results she wanted. "Do you see the railing around the trees? I want to be able to hang custom-made stockings on these while using them to keep people from taking the ornaments off the tree."

"Securing the railings may be a challenge."

"You can't nail them to the floor?"

His expression turned stunned. "This is real hardwood! Do you know how expensive it is—and you want to make holes in it?"

As he crouched to move aside a Moroccan rug and examine the floor more closely, Marina bent over him. "But it's not as if this is going to be temporary. The railing will stay."

"Confident, aren't you?"

"Yes. Do you have a problem with that?"

"It's not my money you're throwing away."

The nerve of the man! "Why are you assuming that I'm going to fail?"

Read rose swiftly, and unaware of how close she was, bumped into her with the full force of his powerful body. Fortunately, his reflexes remained as excellent as she remembered, and he saved her just as she began to topple backward into the furniture, or maybe onto the floor.

He pulled her toward him and used his body to steady her. "Damn my clumsy— I'm sorry."

"It's okay. I shouldn't have, uh..." She couldn't finish because their close proximity made her too aware of him, his stormy eyes, his firm mouth, his even firmer body.

"I should have been more careful," he told her gruffly.

"No, I was crowding you."

Something angry flickered in his eyes. "Do you have to be so agreeable all the time?"

She couldn't believe his reaction. "Would you be happier if I hit you, or maybe just fired you and threw you out?"

"Yeah. Then I could leave here with a clean conscience."

"You can anyway."

"Yeah. Right."

"What's stopping you?"

"Those Bambi eyes of yours," he muttered, his fingers tightening slightly. "The thought of you falling into the hands of some crook who'd ultimately take advantage of you and your inexperience in this area—which shows big-time."

"Is that all?"

"Don't push it, Marina."

But his gaze had lowered to her mouth, and she saw something familiar and exciting in his eyes that she had seen before. Something that filled her dreams for years, and that she had yearned for for too long.

She lifted her chin, yielding to a recklessness that was new to her. "Is it?"

"Not quite," he replied, an instant before claiming her mouth with his.

He didn't want to kiss her. She could feel his anger and resentment, even as his lips pressed against hers and his heat seeped into her. But what made Marina's heart sing was that he couldn't seem to help himself. Overjoyed with that knowledge, she wrapped her arms around his neck and gave herself up to the emotions that had known no outlet for a decade.

He groaned and forced her lips apart, crushed her closer to him. It was as if he was trying to make up for all the lost time in a few explosive seconds, and although she wanted his hunger and passion, wanted his eagerness and energy, she didn't have his experience. That didn't matter to her, but it made an obvious and profound impression on him.

He jerked back his head and frowned at her. "My God . . . it's not possible."

"What?" she asked, a little dizzy.

"You're twenty-eight, for pity's sake. Where's your sense of self-preservation?"

"I don't understand."

"You don't have any experience with men, do you?"

She couldn't resist reaching up to that wonderful mouth she ached to feel again. "I have what you taught me."

He swore under his breath. "That's not funny."

"It wasn't meant to be," Marina replied, seeing no reason not to be utterly truthful. "I told you, I've lived a different life than most women, Read. The only man who's ever held me like this is you. The only man to have ever kissed me as if he wanted to share the very air that fills my lungs is *you*."

"Stop it."

"You want me to lie?"

As if he was fighting his own will, he shifted one hand to cup her face. "I want you to quit sounding as if you think we can pick up where we left off."

"I know that's impossible."

"It is."

Only his fingers kept moving restlessly; he caressed her cheek and inched toward her hair. His gaze continued to roam hungrily over her face.

"It *is*, damn it." And yet he lowered his head and closed his mouth over hers again.

This next kiss was less angry, but that made the ardent assault all the more breathtaking. This time Marina caught a glimpse of Read's grief, the frustration and the desire that had never been consummated. It broke her heart, and she tried to show him that she'd grieved, too; that she'd missed him and the promise of what had blossomed so briefly between them.

With a deep-throated groan, he tore his mouth from hers and forced her to arm's distance. "No more."

Although Marina needed to grip his forearms to steady herself, her voice came calm and sure. "Why not? I like the way you kiss me. I always have."

"That doesn't matter. It can't!"

He almost yelled the protest. As the desperate sound echoed in the room, Read closed his eyes and raked his hands through his hair. Marina would have loved to offer him the consolation of her embrace, to reassure him that she understood his nervousness and doubt. She'd dealt with her own share, only to come to the conclusion that it was saner, healthier, to trust what was in her heart.

"Look," he said quietly, "this was a mistake. It won't happen again."

Not "mustn't," not "can't," but "won't." His resolve stung. It was so foreign from the intimacy they'd just shared, Marina was sure she must have heard incorrectly, and yet his expression told the terrible truth—Read regretted giving in to whatever had driven him to touch her.

"There's a streak of cruelty in you that I don't remember being there before," she whispered, feeling as if she was bleeding from an internal wound.

His jaw worked. "I'm not cruel. I'm just a realist."

"And you flirt with euphemisms."

With an exasperated look, he let her go, spun away from her to gesture around him. "All right, you want it in black and white? Look at this place. It's practically a castle."

"It's a large house. Stately, maybe, but hardly a castle."

"Because you've been in some, haven't you?"

She didn't like what he was driving at. "I can't deny that."

"Well, I haven't."

"Suggesting what?"

"Gold and tin, Marina. Diamonds and glass. Silk and polyester. Take your pick of the contrasts," Read declared, his tone hardening. "It all boils down to the same thing. We're polar opposites. To try to pretend that we're not is asking for trouble, not to mention grief that neither one of us needs or wants. Maybe I was too young and dumb—and, okay, hooked on you—before to acknowledge it, but I've had years to wise up and see things the way they really are.''

His rejection had Marina clutching the notebook to her chest like a shield. ''But I'm not asking you for anything except your expertise in woodworking and the friendship we once shared. Do you want me to pretend I don't miss it?''

''We weren't friends, we were falling in love,'' he insisted, stiffening. ''We would have become lovers if you hadn't left.''

If... if... if... ''I told you, I had no control over what—''

''I *know*,'' he all but roared. ''But you did leave, and that changed everything.''

Marina quickly bit her lower lip to keep it from trembling. ''How true... and your son Ricky is clear evidence of that.''

''Leave him out of this,'' Read snapped. His chest rose and fell, his eyes blazed. ''It's today that matters.''

''How convenient. If I came back penniless and emotionally broken, someone with a bad case of co-dependency, I suppose you would have greeted me more warmly?''

Although there was a moment of guilt in his eyes, he had no trouble rebounding. ''This is nuts. You don't want to hear anything I have to say.''

''On the contrary, I'm very interested.'' Marina took a step closer. ''Most of all I'm interested in why you're here if all you want to do is insult and hurt me.''

''Damn it all, Marina—''

Someone cleared his throat behind her. She spun around to see a man close to her age take off his baseball cap and approach her. Twin dimples punctuated an apologetic but warm smile. A nice-looking man, one she knew she'd never met before.

"Excuse me for interrupting, Read, Ms. Davidov. I'm Seth Fields—my father thought I should introduce myself since I'll be supervising when he can't be here."

So this was Phil Fields's son. His timing couldn't be worse. Not only was Marina not in the mood to have to deal with meeting another new face—no matter how hard she worked at it, meeting new people remained difficult for her—but she was embarrassed by what he might have heard pass between her and Read. Only the fact that she had to keep Read from knowing how deeply he was upsetting her made her return the man's smile and offer her hand.

"Hello, Mr. Fields. I'm very glad to have you and your father handling this project for me."

"Please, make it Seth."

He crossed to her, trim, attractive and cheerful—so American, she thought, feeling anything but herself. It was ridiculous, since she'd been born here, too. But her life had been so different than the lives of everyone she came in contact with. Would the day ever come when she didn't always feel like an outsider?

"Seth it is," she replied, avoiding his admiring look. "I'm Marina—and apparently you know Read Archer."

"From way back. He was the hero of Berryfield High the year I started playing freshman football. How's it going, Read?"

"Fine."

Seth was inches shorter than Read, and his hair was almost as dark as hers, but his cheerful demeanor gave him a bright aura. In contrast, Read seemed sulky.

"Dad said something about you doing the custom work here?"

Read's gaze swung briefly to Marina. "We're discussing that now."

"So I heard. Need any help? I'm a great arbitrator."

"No."

The message behind Read's curt reply was unmistakable, and Seth was clearly not slow. "Then I'm interrupting. Excuse me, I won't take more than a minute of your time. Marina, I just wanted to add that if you have any questions or problems, please don't hesitate to let me know."

"That's very kind, Seth. You seem as conscientious and thorough as your father."

"I better be." He beamed. "Or he'll fire me." He raised a hand in parting and backed from the room. "I'll touch base again later. Marina, I'd like to show you some paint color charts."

"Wonderful," Marina replied, nodding.

Read watched the younger man withdraw, disturbed by his reaction to him, as much as Fields's to Marina. Seth was right; they'd known each other for years. In all that time he'd never had one negative thought about the guy. But the red tide of jealousy that swept through him when Seth's gaze had zeroed in on Marina and his smile had turned as goofy as a teenager's was just another sign to Read that he was probably incapable of behaving objectively around this woman. How he wished she'd stayed away.

"You were saying?"

Marina had turned to him. Her expression was composed, patient; she looked as if she had no idea what she'd done. More than likely, she didn't. He was no whiz at female psychology—Gwenn had pointed that out to him more than once when he'd failed to be sensitive to her moods—but he didn't need to be an expert to know Marina didn't have the capability of acting like a vamp. If she came off as feminine and alluring, it was because that's exactly who she was. That made what had to be said all the more difficult.

"We can't go back."

He hated seeing the flinch at the corners of her eyes, realizing how deep her hurt went. Despite his own hurt, his past anger and present resentment, he still felt for her and believed she was too soft for her own good. How in the world did she hope to open and operate a business, function in the real world, when only minutes ago she'd told him that her past ten years had been as incubated an existence as the first eighteen?

"Read...believe me when I say that more than anything, I have no desire to go backward in time. The very reason that I'm doing this is to go on, to live *my* life, mistakes or no mistakes *my* way."

That was the problem. *Her* way seemed to be to torment him with memories of what they'd once had. He needed to make her refocus elsewhere. "Are you prepared to face the possibility that this—venture might not work out?"

"Are you speaking as an impartial observer, or someone who doesn't know how to admit a project might be too much for him?"

When had she become a politician? The suspiciousness he understood; the day they'd met she'd reminded him of a scared little rabbit ready to slam the door in his face and hide. There were still traces of that wary girl in her. But there was a new stoicism and resolve that hadn't been there before. He had a feeling she already knew what he was up to and wasn't about to let him get away with too much.

"I'm speaking as someone who knows what it is to lose... everything that matters."

She studied him in prolonged silence, and too late he realized why. He hadn't meant for his words to have a double meaning, but he couldn't take them back now.

"Anything worthwhile has its risks and its cost," she finally told him.

"Fine." There was nothing to be gained from continuing to argue with her. He could see his only solution was to give her an estimate that even she couldn't afford. That would settle things, and he could go away and lick his wounds. "Show me the rest and let's get this over with."

She led him to the formal dining room, as big as his kitchen and living room combined. Read couldn't help but admire the exceptional detail work in the room from the monogrammed, slipcovered chairs to the pier glass at the head of the table, to the multitiered chandelier, to the plaster scroll trim along the baseboards and ceilings. The table could easily seat twenty, and there was enough china in the hutch for twice as many.

It had to be the most formal room in the house. "What do you want to do with all this?" he asked, truly at a loss.

"Burn it and start over?"

Certain he'd heard incorrectly, he spun around to focus on her. "Pardon?"

She grimaced. "It's cold and stuffy. I've always hated this room. The windows are fine." She pointed to the wall of floor-to-ceiling glass that ran the length of the room and provided a southern view of the spectacular grounds. "And I like the mirror over the fireplace, but the rest..."

Heaven help him, but the forlorn expression on her face made it impossible to resist asking. "Does it bring back unhappy memories?"

"Of other places, other dinners. Constantly dining with strangers. Eating foods that more often than not didn't agree with you." She shook her head. "We never ate in here. My father took most of his meals in his workroom, or in the kitchen with me if he was relaxed and in the mood for company."

"And who did you eat with the rest of the time?" Read asked in spite of himself.

"No one."

The image of her alone brought an unwelcome pang. "Didn't you have a housekeeper? I distinctly remember someone—"

"Mrs. Pederson always left in the afternoon after her chores to be with her husband, Donald, back in the garage apartment."

By exposing how lonely she'd been, she was chiseling away at his armor and resolve as successfully as if she was using a power drill. More lonely than she'd admitted to him before. Back then she'd confessed that she had trouble making friends because she was shy. At school her classmates thought she was a snob. But she'd liked the teachers. If only one of them could have helped her escape her father's suffocating hold on her. If only *he'd* been given more time...

He cleared his throat and struggled to concentrate on the room. "Next to turning everything into kindling, what did you have in mind?"

"This is where I'd like to show local crafts if I can find enough artisans who are willing—things like nutcrackers, rocking horses, teddy bears, vine and pine reindeers..."

"What will you do with that?" Read pointed to the table.

"I'll offer it to the college, or ask if they know someone who has a need for it."

Quite a gift. He was beginning to understand that her financial situation had to be even healthier than he'd thought, which made him feel gloomier than ever. Maybe as a younger man he'd been too lovesick to see that he could never make her happy, but it was clear now that he didn't have a hope in hell of making an heiress like Marina happy.

To ease the tension those thoughts brought, he wandered around the room. Ironically he could begin to see a hint of what she had in mind for the place, and that made him feel all the grimmer.

If successful, The Christmas House would be a stunning place. However, such an endeavor would require a great deal of work to set up, let alone manage. Too much for one slight woman. Even if she had help, she would have her hands full. That spawned the first hopeful thought he'd had all day—if she was tied up with her business, she wouldn't have time to focus on him—or what had been.

"Read . . . are you going to help me?"

Not "take the job" but "help." He almost groaned, because he wanted, needed her to keep thinking of him as someone she would hire. He'd already compromised himself when he'd kissed her. What would it be like if he had to face her every few days? Could he keep his hands to himself? Ten years ago he'd walked around in a daze at the mere thought of tasting her sweet lips again. His appetite was far stronger now, and it had been denied for a long time.

Marina's smile waned. "We always come back to the past, don't we?"

"Afraid so."

"Do you hate me so much—"

"Let's leave hate out of this." If he couldn't explain his feelings to himself, how could he hope to tell her?

"All right. What else can I say, Read? How can I get you to take this project? Will reminding you about your children help? Mr. Fields said—"

"I'll just bet he did. Well, you can skip that part, too," he muttered, shoving his hands into the pockets of his jacket. "The trouble with living in one community your entire life is that too many damned people like to stick their noses in your business." Damn it, he didn't need her to tell him that he would be a fool to turn her down because of a broken heart and stung pride.

But she was right again. He needed the work. The kids deserved better. No matter what his personal problems were with Marina, he had to think of them first.

"Can you afford me?" he asked, allowing himself a little arrogance.

Marina arched a fine eyebrow. "Name your price."

Chapter Four

He told her yes. But in the days that followed, Marina wondered if she hadn't made a mistake by working so hard to get Read to take her on as a client.

It proved more difficult than she'd anticipated to do anything that required concentration when he was in the house, and for several days she couldn't have avoided him if she'd tried. There was measuring to do, and decisions to be made regarding various wood and stain choices on the pieces of furniture she wanted him to make. She'd known her input would be required, of course, but she'd hoped the tone of their meetings would be more professional, if not congenial. Instead, the tension began as palpable and grew steadily worse.

On the morning he planned to purchase some of the material he would be needing, he stopped at the house first, expecting her to drop everything so he could immediately review his notes and her color choices. He criticized every decision she made, then waited with visible impatience if she took too long to select an alternate.

No one was more relieved than she was when those daily visits ceased. As it was, he left her nerves frayed and her sleep disturbed. Not even the kindness of Phil Fields and his son, Seth, who quickly picked up on the situation and tried to run interference, had eased those awkward moments with Read. She began to wonder if she'd made a mistake hiring him, and wondered if she should ask Phil to recommend someone else.

Then Seth helped her direct her focus elsewhere. "Are you going to be opening the gates for the kids to come trick-or-treating on Halloween?" he asked one afternoon as she picked up a brilliant red maple leaf from the driveway.

She hadn't heard him come out to get something from his truck. "It hadn't crossed my mind. I've been rather preoccupied with Christmas."

"It might be a way to spread the word about your plans for the house. At the least it would get your mind off, er, the business, while you're waiting for us to finish the front room."

He was too nice to actually mention Read, but she saw the concern in his dark eyes. An invitation, too. Grateful for both, she thanked him, and quickly learned he was a sanity saver.

Naturally, having never celebrated the festivity herself, she didn't have a clue as to what to do or where to find decorations. Seth volunteered to drive her around town to see other people's decorations, then took her to several nurseries that stocked what she needed.

She bought dried cornstalks, then bound and stacked them on each side of the front gate, then bought more to design her own scarecrows. When dressing them became a problem, Seth cheerfully took up a collection of old work clothes from among his employees. Next she bought square bales of hay and dozens of pumpkins, which she scattered artistically on and around them. Seth told her that was a good start, but delighted her by painting comical or silly faces on a few.

When he suggested flowers for the long-neglected flower beds, she couldn't resist, although she felt guilty taking so much of Seth's time. "Are you sure you aren't going to get into trouble with your father?" she asked him, as he drove her to yet another garden center.

"He understands that you don't drive," Seth replied with a shrug. "Besides, he likes you. And he knows I do, too." When she failed to respond to that, he teased, "I particularly like the way you talk. You roll your *R*s and emphasize the *CH* more than Americans usually do, and you have a tendency to say *een* instead of *in*."

"It's because we spoke nothing but Russian when my father was alive," Marina told him, once again embarrassed that she stood out as an oddity in her own country.

"Hey, I'm not making fun of you. I think it's sexy."

She couldn't deny it did her ego good to be thought of that way, but it also warned her that she mustn't encourage Seth too much. She couldn't respond to him the way she sensed he wanted, and she didn't want to hurt him by giving him false hope. That was why, when later she realized she needed more plants, she had the nursery deliver her order.

She planted every color of chrysanthemum and pansy available—white, gold, rust, yellow and purple. Once she got them planted, she was caught up in the fever and brought in more pumpkins to line the driveway, all the way to the front door where additional mums and pansies were already filling great copper and brass urns.

"Do you think the children will get the message that they're welcome here?" she asked Phil Fields late one afternoon, as she walked him out to his truck.

He ran his hands over his belly, swollen from the homemade borscht and bread she'd prepared for him and his workers as a thank-you for their kindness to her. "Well, they should. The place looks like a park, as nice as anywhere in town."

With that encouragement, she ordered a taxi a few days later when Phil's crew left for the day, and purchased an assortment of every candy available. Everything that would have appealed to her if she'd been the one going on that night of door-to-door adventuring.

She was paying the taxi and hoisting two full shopping bags from the back of the cab when Read arrived in his pickup truck. Already exhausted from a day of cleaning and other chores, she sighed, wondering if she was going to have to face yet another round of censure from him. She didn't have the energy to fight anymore.

"You take a taxi to shop?" he asked, staring incredulously after the cab as he emerged from his truck.

Once again she repeated her explanation. "I don't have a driver's license."

"Everyone has a driver's license."

"Read."

Her whispered plea reached him with surprising speed. "Excuse me. I'd forgotten that you're different."

The words were by no means meant as an apology, and the sardonic tone annoyed her. "There's also no more Archer grocery store with a deliveryman."

"Thank heaven for small favors," he muttered under his breath. But he did nod at the bags. "Let me have them so you can unlock the door."

"Thank you. I'm quickly discovering that candy weighs more than my schoolbooks used to, and there was a time I believed nothing was heavier or more dull than science and math texts."

As she started up the sidewalk, she heard Read stop in his tracks. Curious, she turned in time to see him staring into the bags.

"This is all candy? What for?"

"Halloween."

"You took a taxi to go shopping for *candy?*"

Trying not to lose her temper completely, Marina went on to unlock the dead bolt and pushed open the front door. "How else was I supposed to get it? That's how I do all of my errands." She decided not to share the news about Seth's helpfulness. Heaven knows what he would find to criticize there, and it was none of his business. "But I am going to sign up for driving lessons as soon as I can leave the premises knowing I won't be needed for an hour or so." She'd been thinking that through for days now, and found the idea of having her own car exciting—although she became terrified when she thought of actually going through the process of purchasing one.

"There's no school near here," Read said, breaking into her thoughts. "The closest is a good hour away."

Marina shrugged. "If it can't be helped, it can't be helped."

"Hell. I'll teach you."

"What?" She stared at him as he passed her and headed for the kitchen. She shut the door and followed.

"I said I'll teach you. You need to learn, and whoever has to drive out here to pick you up for lessons will charge you an arm and a leg just for travel expenses, so I'll teach you. Look at it as my gesture to the community," he added, setting the bags on the center island in the kitchen.

Marina lingered in the doorway of the huge room. "Why?" she demanded simply.

"Because I have a reputation around here as a safe driver."

"Not good enough."

"Believe me, the way most of the people drive in this town, that's a lot."

"You're purposely ignoring my point. Need I remind you that you don't want to spend any more time around me than you have to? What's changed?"

"Nothing."

Maybe he could make a stranger believe that, but not her. When she didn't comment any further, he scowled at her.

"Don't make a big deal out of it. You need to learn, I have a conscience. Isn't that enough?"

The thought of being the beneficiary of that conscience would have made her feel better if it wasn't already putting a trapped look on his face. Dear heaven, he confused her.

"You'll have to let me pay you for your time."

Something dark and violent flared in his eyes. "Don't even think of it. I said I'd do it and that's that."

"But—"

"Change the subject, Marina."

Yes, he was a strange man...and he proved a tougher taskmaster. She realized *that* during her first lesson three days later.

On Saturday he picked her up just before noon, dropped the children off at the movies for a matinee—despite their protests and assurances that they wouldn't mind coming along—then drove to the outskirts of town, away from traffic congestion, where they changed places. Marina quickly learned that few people if anyone could please him.

"Don't talk, just listen. The speed limit is thirty-five, that doesn't mean going fifteen is going to make you brownie points with the officer who'll test you. It's just as dangerous to go too slow as it is to go too fast. Don't assume. Stop and look both ways. Don't change lanes without signaling."

It was a great deal to remember, and she made a mistake quickly. Several of them.

"You're too close to the car in front of you!

"Exactly what do you think a blinking red light means?

"Watch out for the— *Curb.*"

By the time she pulled into the driveway, she was so close to tears, she barely managed to get the truck stopped before leaping from it and running inside. She ignored his shout after her, and then the pounding on the front door, which she'd bolted and leaned against while choking back sobs.

When she heard him leave, she stumbled up the circular staircase to her room and threw herself on her bed, the tears coming fast and furious. Miserable wretch of a man! What right did he have to treat her as if she was still a child, or worse, stupid! What had she done except try her best? She should never have let him talk her into this arrangement. He didn't want to help, he wanted to punish her!

Minutes later the phone rang. She refused to answer it, knowing who it had to be. She'd given Read her number, but she had no intention of talking to him because she couldn't imagine him apologizing and she didn't think she could bear another judgmental remark from someone who'd meant so much to her.

For days afterward, she lived in fear that he might come by and make a scene, but he didn't. When a whole week passed and there was no sign of him, Marina finally relaxed to where she returned to her daily routine, tackling the chore of cleaning the huge house, cooking lunch for the workmen and handling whatever issue came up regarding her fledgling business. The focus on getting her driver's license was put aside for the moment. Maybe the theory of getting back on a horse after you were thrown worked for some, but she wanted some quiet, stress-free time before she tried again.

On Halloween morning, which fell on Saturday, she rose with excitement and dressed in a cashmere tunic the color of fresh pumpkin and black leggings. Adding a vibrant scarf with multicolored fall leaves and copper-and-gold threading, she slipped on gold hoops and practically danced down the stairs. Her mood was a far cry from last week's, and for good reason—today she would get to show the townspeople of Berry-field that the Davidov estate was no longer that curious, closed place it had been for years.

Throughout the day she busied herself filling bowls of candy, then moving them from spot to spot in the foyer. Seth had already told her that trick-or-treating began later in the afternoon, with the younger children arriving just before dusk and the older ones later. Although she was impatient for that time to come, she happily carved several jack-o'-lanterns from some of the biggest pumpkins in her yard, set in sconces with candles and placed them around the front door.

At four o'clock she opened the gates, and at five she switched on the floodlights to highlight her decorations and offer a welcoming path to the front door. Then she turned on the music she'd bought, tapes of comical or melodramatic tunes and Hollywood special-effects soundtracks that were more humorous than spooky to her. She could just imagine how it would have offended her father. He would probably have ripped the tapes to shreds and gone to bed with a bottle of pills to nurse one of his frequent headaches.

At six, she began standing guard at the window nearest the door, wondering if the gates had somehow swung shut in the wind. But there was no wind tonight, and when she rechecked, there was nothing wrong with her doorbell, either. However, she had yet to have her first visitor.

By seven o'clock she turned off the tape player and began blowing out the nearly burned-out candles in the pumpkins. She didn't need anyone to tell her that no one would be coming trick-or-treating to her house.

What had she done wrong? Her decorations were wonderful, her property well lit. She'd tried to do everything she could think of to welcome people.

Too disappointed to focus on anything else, she got her coat and keys. There was no sense staying put and getting herself worked up and upset; she would take a walk and see where the children *were* going.

She headed toward downtown, only a few blocks from her house. Traffic was light, and there were enough houses and streetlights to make her feel comfortable about being alone at this hour. Once or twice she saw a car pause and a load of children rush out and run up to someone's front door. Her chest tightened with envy at the adults enjoying the giggles and yells of children who rushed from one house to the next.

But it was when she approached Berryfield Elementary School that she saw real traffic. Dozens and dozens of cars were parked near the gym, and music and the roar of laughter, screams and chatter rushed out at her whenever the heavy doors swung open and people both tall and small came out. Most of the children were in costume, and each one carried either a plastic pumpkin or a shopping sack filled to the brim with goodies.

As Marina wondered what was going on and whether she should venture inside, the door burst open again and an adorable small lion emerged. Blinded by an overlong mane, it missed the top stair and dove forward. Despite the candy launching at her like missiles, Marina lurched forward to save the child.

In the next instant the door opened again and Read exited with Ricky. "Molly!"

Between the shock of seeing Read again and being knocked to her knees in order to catch hold of the little girl, Marina was left momentarily breathless. Truth be known, she wasn't sure what hurt more, the bruising concrete or having to acknowledge Read's presence. However, the latter was delayed as he hoisted the child off her by the scruff of her neck.

"Young lady, what did I tell you about running off without me?"

"Daddy! You don't pick up a lion this way!"

"You do if she's a mischievous squirt who doesn't behave."

Set on her feet, Molly pushed back the hood of her costume and looked up indignantly, only to spot Marina. "Marina! Look, Daddy," she cried, pointing with her pumpkin, spilling several more pieces of candy. "It's Marina!"

Shoving the container into her father's hands, she spun to Marina and wrapped her arms around her neck. Still on her knees, Marina hugged the child, breathing in the scent of bubble gum, popcorn and the various wonderful smells she linked with childhood.

"Hello, little lion," she murmured, trying to ignore the pang in her heart that was every bit as strong as the sting in her knees.

"Do you like my costume?"

"I've never seen anything grander."

"Did you hear, Daddy?"

Behind them, Read remained silent, but stooped to pick up the dropped goodies. It was Ricky who descended to join them.

"Hi, Marina! What're you doing here?"

"Well, I—"

"Did you see all that I got?" Molly cried, eager to chat.

"And you know what else? They had a magic forest this year with marshmallow mushrooms and licorice vines and whole bunches of other stuff—and you know what? You could eat it! The haunted cave was the best," Ricky added, his face bearing the dark slashes of paint that she'd noticed in magazine ads that football players wear. An oversize jersey with a single digit completed his costume. "You climb up this fake rock and slide down a dark tunnel into a pool full of rubber snakes. Then you wait for girls to come down and scare them to pieces."

Molly shook her head vehemently, her oversize cub ears wiggling like watery pancakes. "Not me! I was too little. Daddy said I shouldn't go."

Having no idea what they were talking about, Marina looked at Read. He'd finished collecting his daughter's treats, and there was no missing that his silence was as speaking as the children's enthusiasm.

"Is this a school party of some kind?" she asked.

"Halloween Fest. More and more parents feel it's safer to bring their kids to some organized and supervised function like this than take chances having their kids on the street taking candy from strangers.''

Was that why no one had come to her place? She could have saved herself considerable disappointment if *someone* had told her. After sending him a cool look, she focused on the children. ''I didn't realize.'' Struggling to her feet, she summoned a smile for the children. ''So obviously you two had a wonderful time?''

''Yeah, and now we're going to the ice-cream store, right, Daddy?'' Molly cried, hopping up and down with unbridled excitement.

''Guess so,'' Read murmured. ''Since you won't be happy until you have a tummy ache.'' But he was watching Marina and frowning. ''What's wrong? Did you hurt yourself?''

''Not really. I just stumbled when I caught Molly.''

Clearly not believing her, he passed Molly's bucket to Ricky and came down to join her on the bottom stair. Without asking for permission he stooped to inspect her legs. ''The material's not ripped, but that doesn't mean you're not bleeding.''

''It's just a bump. I'll be fine.''

''There could be tendon or ligament damage.''

''I'm *fine*.'' Didn't he understand that she didn't want him touching her? His closeness just reminded her of how insensitive he'd been the other day, and she would be darned if she would cry before him again.

''Maybe you'll feel better after some ice cream,'' Molly said, her voice tiny and sad.

The statement caught her by surprise and she stared. ''Oh, I—''

"Uh, Marina doesn't—" Read said at the same moment.

Ricky stepped forward and grabbed her hand. "Yes, come!"

"Then it'll be a real party, not just us." Molly brushed her tousled curls aside to look up at her father. "Daddy, do you have money for her to have ice cream, too?"

Read looked up into the star-filled sky. Marina would have chuckled at his comical reaction to the child's unabashed honesty if they'd been on more pleasant terms. As it was, she felt obliged to be gracious.

"That's very generous, Molly and Ricky, but I was only out for a short walk. It wasn't my intention to intrude."

"You can be *my* date," Ricky interjected, patting his jacket pocket. "I have a whole month's allowance saved."

Just as Marina sent the boy a loving smile, Read laid a hand on his shoulder.

"That's nice, son, but I said this was my treat, remember?" His gaze sought Marina's. "You're welcome to join us."

"I don't want to," she whispered as low as possible so only he would hear.

"I know...and I know why. And all I can say is that I'm sorry."

"This isn't fair, Read."

"No. So don't come for me." He glanced at his children, who stood by watching them in confusion and worry. "Come for my kids."

"All right."

Read barely registered Marina's reply before Molly whooped and took off running into the parking lot. With a shout of rebuke, her older brother gave chase. That left Read and Marina to bring up the rear. As she turned, he noticed her wince, and he took hold of her arm. Immediately she stiffened.

"Marina, don't."

"You knew what I was doing for Halloween. You could have warned me. Why didn't you?"

"Because if I had been wrong and people had swarmed to your place with their kids, you would have seen me as a party pooper."

"Ah...and you're happy with being only a semi-party-pooper?"

She'd made her point. Again. But this time his annoyance was only secondary to his chagrin. "I'm sorry I let you go through so much trouble for nothing."

A strange smile curved her lips. "Oddly enough the experience wasn't wasted. I enjoyed the preparations, and that's how I realized they were part of what the festivities are about."

"Keep it up, you're going to put us all to shame."

"I'm just trying to learn."

They'd reached the truck. Read unlocked the passenger side and Ricky and Molly climbed into the back seat. As Marina got in front, Read realized that despite his concern for her fall, despite his shame for his earlier behavior, he really was glad that she'd agreed to come with them. How to communicate that was another story.

There was no chance to say anything during the drive to the Polar Express, the ice-cream shop in the center of town. Molly was her talkative self, and Ricky seemed to have been bitten by the chatterbox bug, as well.

"I'm gonna have the biggest hot-fudge sundae," Molly declared, shortly after updating Marina on what else she'd consumed at the Halloween Fest.

"Yeah, right," Ricky replied with a senior sibling's disdain. "You couldn't eat half of one if Dad kept you on bread and water for a week."

"Can so! I'll eat two if I want."

"Good idea," Read drawled. "Then we'll have to roll you home. I've always wanted my very own roly-poly girl."

"Daddy!" Molly squealed, covering her face but clearly delighted with her father's teasing.

"Dad, can I get the Cliffhanger?"

As Read groaned, Marina glanced from him to Ricky and asked, "What's the Cliffhanger?"

"It's the biggest dessert on earth," Ricky crowed. "You start with this big ol' brownie, and then stack all this Rocky Road ice cream on top, then whipped cream, then marshmallow and chocolate sauce, and nuts and a cherry."

"And you have to try to eat it before it falls all over the table and everyone around you," Read added as an aside.

Ricky echoed his father's earlier protest. "Aw, Dad, it's neat. Marina, you should try one, too."

"Well, as exciting as it sounds, unless this is an all-night establishment, I'm not sure I could eat a whole one in a single sitting. Would you believe that in my whole life I only remember one scoop of vanilla on a cone?''

"*What?*" both Ricky and Molly gasped.

Whispers of "unreal" and "awful" drifted from the back seat. Marina chuckled. "Actually, it's a marvelous memory. I got to watch the woman make it before my very eyes after a day of hiking in the Alps. It tasted what I imagined clouds must taste like."

"No, they taste like cotton candy," Ricky said, all seriousness.

"Oh, dear. Well, I've never tasted that."

"Daddy!" Molly leaned forward against her seat belt. "Marina's never tasted cotton candy!"

"As far as I know I still have twenty-twenty hearing, pumpkin."

"But, Daddy—the circus is coming soon and you said we could go. Maybe Marina can come with us. They have cotton candy at the circus."

"The circus isn't until nearly summer, honey."

"Is that right after Valentine's Day?"

Read shot Marina an apologetic look. "We don't usually tell time by holidays where you receive gifts." That's all he needed, to have her think he raised his kids to be materialistic. As it was, they were inching dangerously close to that matchmaking scheme again—just when he'd begun to hope they were cured. To change the subject he suggested, "How about singing Marina the song you learned tonight."

Instead they told dreadful knock-knock jokes that Marina couldn't possibly have found entertaining. And yet somehow she laughed—and not polite laughter, either. No, she actually seemed to find them funny.

After Read parked in front of the store and he and Marina followed the children inside, he couldn't resist wiping away the tear of laughter he spotted at the corner of her left eye. "Don't spoil them. You'll make them impossible to live with."

"You're very lucky," she replied, drawing away from him slightly. "They're born charmers."

"They don't get it from me, do they?"

Inside they found that the kids had claimed their favorite booth, the one in the corner by the window that looked out at the park. Next to studying the picture menu, they enjoyed eyeing the pond in the middle of the park best. A family of ducks lived there, thoroughly spoiled by the community. But what surprised Read was that both kids were in the same side of the booth. Usually they gravitated to opposite sides. "Girl cooties," was Ricky's typical judgment. "Boy crud," was Molly's. Read knew why they'd suddenly abandoned their sibling rivalry, and it confirmed his suspicion that Marina was once again their prime "Mommy" target. He had to figure out how to stop them before they embarrassed her.

"Are you planning to deal with getting ice cream and whatnot on that game shirt?" he asked his son, nodding from him to his accident-prone daughter.

"Sure, Dad. No problem. I'll take care of her."

Read couldn't help but raise an eyebrow. His boy's casual acceptance was nowhere near the way he usually reacted, but he wasn't about to make a production out of this in front of Marina. Clearing his throat, he invited her to take her seat in the booth. Maybe it would make things easier, he thought, as he slid in beside her. If they didn't have to sit across from one another, their eyes wouldn't keep locking, their knees wouldn't keep bumping, and maybe he could swallow something without feeling as if he had to force it past a closed drawbridge in his throat.

But it didn't take long to realize that no matter what their seating arrangement, his size made a booth problematic. Instead of their knees bumping, their thighs touched. Instead of getting to stare into her eyes, he had to deal with their arms rubbing. And her hair kept wrapping itself around him like fingers, making him wish it was his bare flesh it was caressing. He could tell Marina noticed, too, because the prettiest blush rose and stayed permanently in her cheeks.

"Sorry," he murmured, shifting yet again after they'd placed their order.

"It's all right." But once again Marina tried to sweep her ebony mane over her left shoulder.

Molly stared with unabashed wonder. "How long do you think it'd take me to get my hair that long, Marina?"

"Oh, another year or so. But you may not like it. It takes a great deal of brushing."

"That's okay. Daddy likes to do that, don't you, Daddy?"

"Absolutely." He nodded, careful to keep a poker face. "Next to sticking my arm down a lion's throat, I can't think of anything more fun."

The children got a big kick out of that. But Marina eyed Molly with continued interest.

"I have a silver comb and brush set that had been my mother's. If you'd like to visit me sometime, we can use it to do your hair."

"Can I, Daddy?" Molly gushed, clasping her hands prettily.

Read thought of a few choice things he wanted to tell Marina. "We'll see. Miss Davidov doesn't realize what a pest you can be."

"I'd be happy to watch her, Dad," Ricky said, focusing on rolling and unrolling his napkin. "You know, kinda like baby-sitting. But you wouldn't have to pay me anything."

Rather than answer, Read turned to Marina. "These are not my children. I think they're pod people from Mars. They must have assumed Ricky and Molly's identity." Then as everyone giggled, he leaned across the table and softly demanded, "Whoever you are, bring my kids back! I miss not hearing them blowing out my eardrums, and wheedling me for favors and treats."

"Daddy, it's us," Molly said, patting his hand. "We're just being friends with Marina 'cuz she doesn't have any, right, Marina?"

"Exactly...thank you very much. Both of you," she said to the children. "And I want you to know you're welcome to visit anytime."

Read sobered. He knew Marina meant well. He also realized she had to be lonely in that big place she lived in. However, she didn't realize what such invitations would do to his kids. And him. One day she would meet someone of her own kind, start her own family.

Neither he nor his children needed any more heartbreak in their lives.

As the waitress brought their order and the children exclaimed over theirs, Marina leaned closer to him, as if she'd sensed his unrest.

"You needn't look so grim. I don't intend to upset your life."

That's what she thought, he brooded. She already had. She had for years.

Chapter Five

Under the circumstances, Read wouldn't hear of not driving Marina home, and the trip to her house was far more quiet. Full and sleepy, the children slumped in the back seat, contentedly looking out their windows, clutching their collection of Halloween treats. Their only sounds were yawns and an occasional soft humming of a favorite song. Like Marina, Read didn't say a word the entire way.

When he pulled into her driveway and saw all the decorations, though, he experienced another pang of guilt for not having told her something about Berryfield. "I'll walk you to the door," he murmured upon stopping. He had to at least do that.

Leaving the engine idling so the heater would keep the children warm, he listened to Marina whisper goodbyes to them. Then he waited for her to round the truck and followed her up the walkway.

"I'm glad you're not limping," he told her. "How do you feel?"

"A little sore, but fine."

The place was well lit; nevertheless, when she unlocked the door, she immediately reached inside to key in a code to adjust the alarm system. That underscored how alone she was here.

"Would you like me to look around before I go?"

"It's not necessary," she said, running her finger along a series of green lights. She faced him again. "It's a good security system. Thank you for tonight, Read."

He shook his head. He knew full well he didn't deserve her gratitude.

"Yes. Thank you for being so kind to me."

She made him feel like a heel. "You're very easy to be kind to."

"Does that mean you don't hate me anymore?"

The lights above and behind her created a nimbus around her head, and Read knew she'd never looked more beautiful to him. "I never hated you, Marina. I tried, but... I just hurt." Hurt because he'd lost her. Hurt still because he could never have her.

"Me, too. How do we make it stop?"

He didn't know. All he understood was that he wanted to kiss her, to take her in his arms and hold her tight, until the aching stopped. The problem was that tempting himself would only bring worse pain... and heartache to his children.

After a long moment he simply shook his head and began backing away. "I don't know if we ever will."

* * *

"I don't know if we ever will."

Marina blinked at Phil Fields. His words were so much like what Read said a few days ago, that for a moment she lost track of time and what they'd been conversing about. "Excuse me?"

"Finish with our pumpkins. At our house, my wife just wraps some lights around them and they become part of the Christmas decorations." He chuckled and gestured in a way that encompassed the entire yard. "The thing is that they're definitely part of Thanksgiving, so why not leave everything as it is, and enjoy it? Folks don't actually decorate for Christmas until then anyway."

Before she could respond, Read's pickup pulled into the driveway. Marina's heart gave an excited leap. "Uh...thank you, Mr. Fields. I think I'll follow your advice."

"Of course, when you are ready to put up your Christmas stuff, you just let Seth know," the contractor added, following her gaze. "He'd be glad to help you out. We wouldn't want you overloading any fuses or anything. Well...looks as if Archer's as good as his word. He told me yesterday that he would have a piece or two to deliver to you soon."

That was more than he'd said to her. In fact Marina hadn't heard from him since Halloween, to be exact. She followed Phil to Read's truck, hoping her excitement didn't show too much.

Read exited and nodded to the contractor, then her.

"Good to see you," Phil said, slapping him on the back and beaming at the round table in the bed of the truck. "That's a beauty."

"It is, Read," Marina added, impressed at the gleaming creation. "It will look wonderful in the front room."

"Glad you like it."

He spoke politely, but his eyes avoided hers. When he quickly asked Phil to help him carry the table inside, Marina was left to simply stand by and listen to a conversation that centered around sports. Her only chance to say anything else was after she showed them how she wanted the piece set in the parlor. Right after they set down the table, Phil got called into another room by one of his men, leaving her alone with Read.

"Did you bring an invoice so I can write you a check?" She wanted to know if it had been Phil's presence that had made him hesitant about talking to her.

"It's in the truck, but there's no rush. I have some shelves to put up, too. Just ignore me, because I'll be a while."

Pretend he wasn't there? Impossible. However, she understood what he was telling her; he wanted their relationship to get back on a more professional basis. With a slow nod, she murmured, "Call if you need me," and withdrew.

She spent the day going through a new shipment of inventory, more of the crystal angels she planned to hang on the artificial tree she had just set in the foyer earlier that morning. The detail work of making tiny price tags and attaching them to each item proved painstaking, and Marina was surprised when—after hearing the doorbell—she glanced at her watch and realized it was after three o'clock.

She experienced another surprise when she discovered Molly and Ricky were her callers. "Why, this is a wonderful surprise!"

"After I picked up Molly at day care, I realized I forgot my key this morning. We can't get into the house," Ricky told her, looking anything but regretful. "Dad said he'd be here today, so we thought we'd come get his."

"I thought you said she would ask us to stay, Ricky?" Molly asked, gazing at her brother with great confusion.

"Absolutely, because you've been doing a great deal of walking. Come in, both of you." She hugged them one by one and added a kiss for Molly's wind-reddened cheek.

"I thought I recognized your voice," Read said from behind her. She turned to see him frowning. "What are you guys doing here?"

Ricky explained again—only this time he looked less confident about his story. Read's expression told Marina he didn't buy it for a second.

"Uh-huh. Your key that you keep in your wallet, right?"

"Uh...I left my wallet home, too. It was a real bummer, 'cuz I missed lunch and everything," his son replied, sliding a look to his sister. "Listen, Dad, we can wait for you. We don't mind, do we, Molly?"

Although the little girl shook her head in vigorous agreement, Read narrowed his eyes. "Oh, no, you don't. You aren't going to bother Miss Davidov—"

Marina was glad for the opening. "They're no bother at all. Besides, Read, didn't you hear him? He has to be starved. They probably both are."

"Thirsty," Molly said, sticking out a tongue as pink as her cheeks and proceeding to pant like a puppy.

"Heaven save me from impostors," Read growled.

But Marina caught the twinkle in his eyes and the twitch around his mouth. She herded the children toward the kitchen. "Why don't you come with me. I have some of the prettiest cookies you've ever seen that an acquaintance sent from Europe. I bet they would taste especially good with some hot chocolate."

"All right!" the children cried in unison.

First, however, Marina helped them off with their jackets and hung them over the banister at the foot of the stairs. She smiled as they oohed and aahed over what she'd been working on.

"Wait until you see the tree finished—all of the house," she told them.

"I wish we could," Ricky replied, adding an adult sigh. "But Dad's not likely to let us back."

"Why do you say that?"

"We've known him a long time. You can tell by his face."

They were a delight. "We'll have to figure something out," she told them. Once Read saw how well the children behaved here, and how much she enjoyed their company, surely he would change his mind. Brightening, she clapped her hands together. "Why don't we turn this into a tea party? Without the tea, of course."

"Then how can it be a tea party?" Molly demanded, her face scrunched into a pixie's frown.

"I'll show you."

She had them help her arrange ⟨...⟩ center island, and then brought out ⟨...⟩ mats and silverware. Molly's eyes went w⟨...⟩ saw the china with the gold trim. Marina ⟨...⟩ help her carry things, chuckling to herself as he m⟨...⟩ as if carrying explosives.

She let them both light a set of candles for their centerpiece with a lighter, and then arrange the cookies on a crystal platter. Marina supervised, while heating the milk for their drinks. Through it all, she entertained them with stories about the items they held.

"Those dishes once belonged to cousins of the Czar of Russia. Isn't it wonderful how the firebird's tail becomes the handle of the cup?"

"I thought it was a peacock," Ricky said, eyeing his more closely.

"The firebird is a favorite creature in Russian fairy tales. Molly, that candelabra was a gift to my father from the Countess Molinari. She lives in Venice."

"You knowed a countess?" the little girl gasped. "That's almost as good as a princess! Did she live in a castle? Was she scary to talk to?"

"A villa. It's not quite as big as a castle, and the countess was very sweet and—*normal* is the word you'd probably understand best—just like you and me."

"Wow, what kind of marshmallows is that?" Ricky asked as she shut off the mixer.

After pouring the hot chocolate into the cups he'd brought her, she scooped a large dollop of the white froth on top of each. "Whipped cream. I'm afraid I'm

...s, but I think you'll

...However, he was the
...ping her carry the drinks
...took their seats.

...ll the time?'' Molly whis-
...s she surveyed their bounty.
...o answer carefully. She didn't
...to get the wrong impression.

"W... ...ave here?'' she began thoughtfully. "M... ...okies. But presentation makes it
look more spec... doesn't it? A pretty cup and a lit
candle...''

"Tell me about it,'' Ricky replied. "We get chipped
plastic served on vinyl—when Dad remembers place
mats. It's nothing like this.'' He looked at the cookies. "Um... can we taste now?''

"Absolutely.'' Marina invited him and Molly both
to help themselves. "Why don't you tell me what your
favorite foods are?''

"Mac'roni and cheese!''

"Hot dogs and fries!''

"Oh, dear,'' Marina replied, laughing behind her
cup. "Would you believe I've never tasted either?''

"You must've had a strange life,'' Molly offered,
breaking open her cookie to lick the coffee cream inside.

"Well... different.''

"What did you eat?'' Ricky asked her, reaching for
a chocolate-dipped wafer.

"It depends where we were. For instance Russian
cooking, which my father preferred, is fairly plain and

...bar stools around the
...French lace place
...ide when she
...t Ricky
...ved

91

filling. Caviar...sturgeon eggs," she explained, when she realized they hadn't heard of it before.

Both children screwed up their faces.

"Also boiled eggs. Herring."

"At the same time?" Molly mumbled, her mouth full.

Marina grinned. "It's an acquired taste. But what's interesting is that the eggs are peeled and often marinated in red beet juice. Can you imagine having Easter eggs year-round?"

Ricky shook his head and admitted that wasn't a bad idea. "But I can't even imagine trying herring."

"It's an acquired taste. I'd bet you'd like the blintzes, though."

"What are they?"

Marina used both hands to create a big circle. "Large pancakes that you fill up with all sorts of things like cottage cheese, sour cream and jam."

"I guess that wouldn't be too bad," Molly murmured. "But I think I like mac'roni better."

Grinning, Marina replied, "Maybe next time you can come over we'll try that."

"Promise?"

"Don't get greedy," Read said from the doorway.

Marina almost spilled her drink, and despite the tone in his voice that warned her that he was a bit annoyed, she managed a bright, "Hello. Did you change your mind about joining us?"

"Uh—no. I was just concerned that they were making pests of themselves."

"Not us, Daddy!"

"We're doing good, Dad, aren't we, Marina?"

Nodding to both Ricky and Molly, she turned to their father. "We're having a lovely time, Read. Come, have a cookie at least. You won't compromise your principles by having one cookie." She was teasing him, but gently.

"No, thanks. I just wanted you to know I'm done for now, and to tell the kids that we'll be leaving in ten minutes or so. As soon as I collect my tools."

"But, Daddy, we just started," Molly cried. "Look—the candles aren't even melted yet!"

Marina bit her lower lip to keep from laughing. Oh, Read's child was a treasure; both of them were. She could see that this little party meant as much to them as it did to her. She hoped Read could, too, and wasn't so closed-minded and resentful toward *her* as to discount that.

As if she'd spoken out loud, he turned back toward the door. "Why don't you just let me know when you're done, and I'll check on a few things with Ph— Mr. Fields."

He left before Marina could think of a way to stop him. As the door swung shut, she felt a small hand touch hers.

"Don't be sad," Molly coaxed. "He gets like that if he really likes you."

"Excuse me?" Marina said, with a brief, embarrassed laugh.

"Yeah," Ricky seconded. "He tries to pretend he doesn't care, but you can tell he does."

"Really? I suppose you have to know him better to be able to tell."

"Yeah." Molly nodded sagely. "We've known him all our life."

"Oh, Molly... I do like you. I like you both very, very much."

When Read heard Marina's soft, melodious laugh, he was reminded of the old saying about listening in on others' conversations. He deserved this, all right. Never mind that he was trying to do the right thing and not take advantage of her; any guy less responsible and principled would be working overtime to make her remember how close they'd been ten years ago. Anyone else would have gone in for the kill with a line like, "For old times' sake," and be visualizing a cozy future for himself. But not him.

He had his pride. Regardless of how badly his kids wanted a new mother, he needed to be the one who would provide for his family. No matter what Marina said or did to try to convince him that her wealth didn't mean much to her, he knew it was all she knew; therefore it had to count. All that fancy dishware and silver was perfect proof of it.

Grim but resolute, he sought relief by throwing himself into his work. He spent long hours in his garage workshop, pausing only to prepare the kids' meals, check Ricky's homework and supervise their baths before he tucked them into bed. Afterward, he returned to the shop to continue. Now that he had the parlor ready, he was working on the railing for the living room display.

His kids were no help at all. At every opportunity they tormented him with anecdotes about Marina, or with questions.

"D'you know what, Daddy? She can ride horses," Molly gushed, her expression rapt. "Not cowboy horses like on TV, but like a lady where you wear gloves and hats and shiny black boots. She's gonna show me pictures someday.''

''There was this monster kinda pot on the counter, Dad, only real fancy,'' came Ricky's interjection. ''I thought it was where she kept her dad's ashes or something, but she told me it's a—a sammy something. Oh, yeah, a samovar. Bet you didn't know I knew any Russian. Know what it's used for? Tea. Cool, huh? And she showed me the cups they use. They're glass in these neat silver holders. Marina said next time we come over she would show us how it worked.''

''Daddy, d'you have any friends in Europe? I sure did like those cookies.''

''I feel sorry for her being in that big house all by herself. Do you suppose she gets lonely, Dad?''

On and on it went. A conspiracy. Read knew what his kids were up to; their plan was to drive him out of his mind. But he did manage to stay away from Marina's for nearly another full week. Only, inevitably, it came time to deliver the railing.

He arrived one morning when Marina was saying goodbye to a middle-aged woman in a fur-lined suit. The elegant woman managed to pass within inches of him, yet ignored him as if he didn't exist. Drolly amused, Read watched her slink into a low barracuda of a car and drive away.

''That's Mrs. Danforth-Wellington,'' Marina said, joining him at his truck. ''She's the president of the ladies' art league.''

''Not exactly the friendly type.''

"Yes...and I think I did something unwise by turning down her invitation to join the organization."

Read lifted an eyebrow. "Sounds smart to me if she's representative of the rest of the group."

"But it came to me afterward that she knows a great number of people who could help get the word out about The Christmas House."

That earned her a stare from him. She looked particularly mature and stunning in a deep red dress that he guessed might be cashmere. With its high collar secured at the side of the throat by a pearl button, and matching pearl studs running along the left side of the dress, she stood as a strong representative of her ancestors. But what she'd just said...

"You'd suffer the company of snobs like that to sell a few ornaments?"

Her gorgeous brown eyes lit with gold fire. "Thank you for sharing your feelings about my business, Read. If you'll excuse me, Seth is waiting for me. He's trying to get his people to finish up today, and he needs me to okay something. I don't want to delay him any more than I already have."

As he watched her walk away, her high heels clicking lightly on the sidewalk, Read had to fight the urge to run after her and apologize. Lord knows, he deserved her cold shoulder and more. Since when did he belittle anyone else's efforts to make a go of a business? His inner conflict over the woman was turning him into someone he no longer recognized.

But didn't she see? He knew people like Mrs. What's-her-name; they always managed to get more than they gave. He'd experienced that when his parents owned their business, and even today in his own. He suspected the woman wanted Marina's celebrity, but it was doubtful she would ever come here to shop, no matter what she promised.

Shaking his head, he began carrying the first set of railings inside. Marina had been so preoccupied with her visitor that she'd ignored what he'd brought. That hurt *his* feelings; but once inside the living room, he saw how much work she'd done since the last time he'd been here, and that changed his attitude to one of shame.

"I wanted to have the trees up so that you could install the railings without having to worry about how to maneuver around them," Marina said, coming in behind him. She paused beside him and touched the gleaming, walnut-stained wood. "This is lovely. You were right about the shade. It's going to blend in well."

"Yeah. If you'd gone any lighter, things might have looked too... Marina." He considered her profile and felt his heart clench at the sight of her sad smile. "Marina, I was a jerk about what I said."

"No, you're right. I'm an amateur, and all this might be a pipe dream. But, Read, try to understand—the only way I survived the loneliness and longing all these years has been by dreaming."

She was turning him inside out. It was all he could do not to sweep her into his arms to relieve his frustration and pain. His mouth was dry from wanting to taste hers again.

He swallowed hard. "At some point we have to stop. We have to look at the world the way it really is."

"Grow up, you mean?"

Her dry tone of voice had him glancing at her again. "I'm not suggesting you're immature. Just..."

"Idealistic." Marina tilted her head and studied him with greater curiosity. "How can you have two beautiful children like yours and not be the same way? Their future lies in your ability to hope for a better world for them."

"That's different."

"How convenient to think so."

He uttered a guttural sound. "Believe me, it's neither convenient nor easy."

To his amazement she smiled.

"What's so funny?"

"I'm realizing what a liar you are."

Before he could respond, she quickly, lightly touched her lips to the corner of his mouth. Even as he reached for her, he sensed her stiffening. Following her gaze over his shoulder, he saw Seth leaving the room.

"Excuse me," Marina murmured, and went after him.

What the hell... ? Read wondered.

Marina hurried after Seth. She'd thought they'd finished their business. She'd approved the hardware for the doors on the office behind the checkout counter. The final bill would be mailed by his father. There had been no reason for him to seek her out; instead he'd walked in on a personal moment between her and Read, and the expression on his face told her that she needed to speak with him.

"Seth." She caught up with him outside.

He stopped on the walk and frowned. "It's cold. You shouldn't be out here without a coat."

"Will you come inside with me so we can talk?"

"It's not necessary, Marina. You don't owe me an explanation."

"Seth." She pleaded to him with her eyes. "I'm sorry for not being more clear about Read."

"I should have guessed." He shrugged and offered a sheepish smile. "You can't blame a guy for hoping."

"I do like you."

"I like you, too. But I'm beginning to think our friend Archer isn't playing with a full deck of cards." Seth nodded toward the house. "What's his problem? Would you like to talk about it?"

"It's a long, complicated story, and it barely makes sense to me. I'm not sure I could explain it to you, nor would it be fair to Read to talk about him behind his back."

Seth whistled softly. "Tell him for me that he's a fool if he lets you slip through his fingers."

"Read doesn't pay a great deal of attention to what I say."

"Would you like me to offer him some advice?" Seth asked, his eyes twinkling despite his sad smile.

"Thank you, but no."

"Going to take your chances on wearing him down with gentleness?" He sighed and shook his head. "I wish you luck, Marina. That's a brick wall you're dealing with."

"I know, Seth." But what she couldn't tell him was that she loved that stubborn man. Until she could learn to stop caring, all she could do was hope he stopped rejecting what she instinctively knew he felt for her.

* * *

Read struggled to ignore his curiosity about Seth and Marina the rest of the morning and well into the afternoon. He was two-thirds of the way through with the installation of the railing when he heard a commotion at the other side of the house. Then there was the brief stampede of small feet. "Hi, Daddy!"

"Hey, Dad."

He spun around and whipped off the protective glasses he'd been using during drilling. "What's this?"

"We came to see Marina," Molly said, aiming a wet smack on his left cheek. She waved a cut-and-paste picture inches before his nose. "I wanted to bring her the turkey I made today. You don't mind if I give her the first one instead of you, do you, Daddy? She don't have any little kids to make pictures for her 'frigerator."

"Doesn't," he said automatically. "She *doesn't* have any kids. And it's *re*frigerator."

Ricky put a protective arm around his sister. "Don't be so hard on her, Dad. She knows. She's just excited to be here. Uh... the railing looks good."

Read sat down on the floor and pinched the bridge of his nose. His not-yet-nine-year-old son was using psychology on *him?* This was perfect. He looked over their wind-tousled heads to see Marina in the doorway. She'd changed into a pants and sweater outfit in blue and green, and her smile made it clear she was as happy to see his kids as they were to be here.

"I suppose now that you're here you'll want to hang around until I'm ready to leave?" he drawled, already knowing the answer. He knew Ricky had a key; he'd checked with his son this morning.

"On account I broke my shoe, Daddy." Molly lifted her foot, showing him the snapped lace on her hot pink sneakers. "The sidewalk tripped me."

"Ah." Read looked from the tiny foot to Marina. "Now I'm supposed to ask you if this is infringing on your time."

"It's not," she said sweetly. "We're going to start bringing ornaments and things into the front room after we have a snack. Can we get you anything?"

Aspirin. He was developing a headache, because he knew full well what she was doing. "No, thanks." He did, however, give each of his children meaningful looks. "Now hear this—behave."

For almost half an hour things were fairly quiet. It made him wonder what they were up to in the kitchen. But then a short time later he began hearing squeals and loud voices. Since he was finished with his work for this visit, he followed the sounds to the front parlor where he found his son, daughter and Marina sitting on the floor surrounded by boxes upon boxes of ornaments and gift items.

"This is the most *beautiful*." Molly reverently stroked a porcelain reindeer wearing a fine gold chain with a tiny bell hanging from its neck.

"You said that about the bear ornament," Ricky chided, wearing a necklace of price tag labels.

"That's because I didn't see this one yet. Do you think this is Dancer or Prancer, Marina?" the little girl asked, once again stroking the sleek figurine.

About to answer, Marina spotted him. "Oops, I think we concerned your father again."

"No, I—" Read heard the subtle teasing in her voice and changed his mind. She was right; he had charged in here to look for an excuse to end their visit. He'd been about to punish them because of his inability to reconcile his feelings with her. "I thought you might like to see how the finished product looks," he said quickly before he could change his mind.

Marina brightened. "Let's go look! I could use some advice about setting up some things."

The children rose with care, more care than Read had ever seen them use around their own possessions, let alone anyone else's. Then Molly bolted for him and asked for a piggyback ride. Glad not to be left out of this scenario despite their obvious manipulation of him, he crouched to let her hop on and carried her to the next room. Ricky raced ahead and screeched to a halt before the semicircle of trees inside the new wooden barricade.

"Wow! This is so cool, it's just like a penned-in forest!"

"The finish is still setting, Rick," Read warned quietly. "Be careful."

The boy looked ready to climb onto it, and gingerly backed off. "Sure, Dad. You did good."

"Think so? Thanks. I'm pleasantly pleased myself."

"It is wonderful, Read. Thank you." Marina stopped beside him. "It's exactly what I had in mind."

He couldn't see how. Actually, all he could focus on was that her arm was touching his. It was a reminder of the whispery caress she'd bestowed upon him earlier...and the way she'd taken off after Seth. What had happened between them? What was she up to now?

He cleared his throat. "Are you sure this is what you wanted?"

"Exactly what I wanted! Can't you see it—the trees decorated, baskets of ornaments against the railing and stockings hanging from the posts?"

"Sure sounds like a lot of work, Marina," Ricky said, nodding as if he could see it. "Especially since you said you would be interviewing soon for help. That takes time, too. Me'n Molly could help you until you found some grown-ups, if you wanted us to."

Read laid a hand on his son's shoulder, knowing exactly what the boy was up to; after all, it was only yesterday that he'd overheard him agree with his sister that Marina was "the one." "Now, Rick, Marina doesn't need any—"

"Ricky, that's a marvelous idea," Marina cried before he could get the rest of his explanation out. "You wouldn't mind? But one thing—I certainly would insist on paying you for your time."

As she looked from one excited child to the other, Read set his hands to his hips. "Wait a minute."

"I'm serious," Marina assured him. "It's a wonderful idea, and why shouldn't the children get compensated for their time and efforts?" She beamed at them. "It'll be good practice for when you're grown, not to mention coming in handy for Christmas shopping."

Read couldn't bring himself to argue with her logic. Everything she said was reasonable, except that when he looked down the road and saw his children spending more time with her, *him* spending more time with her, it triggered all the old pains and angsts.

"Please, Daddy? It's about Christmas," Molly murmured, her lower lip beginning to protrude.

He sighed and threw up his hands. "Okay! Fine! I know when I'm outnumbered." Then he wagged a finger at a grinning Ricky. "But if this intrudes on homework—"

"It won't, Dad. Cross my heart."

As Molly clapped and jumped up and down with glee, Marina mouthed thank-you to him. Their gazes clung even after he realized he should look away.

This couldn't work. His mind kept telling him so. But another part of him took too much pleasure and strength from the moment. Just being with her gave him something rare and fulfilling. If he wasn't careful, it was going to turn into full-fledged need.

He didn't quite succeed in matching her smile, but he managed a quiet, "You're welcome."

Chapter Six

Marina could hardly wait for Ricky and Molly to ring her doorbell the next afternoon. Their enthusiasm for what she was doing with the house compounded her own, making her feel as excited as a child again. Not surprisingly, their arrival was noisy.

She welcomed them with bear hugs and listened to them simultaneously tell about their day as she helped them off with their coats. Then it was on to the kitchen for a snack.

"I can't tell you how glad I am to have your help," she told them, when they finally descended on the mass of boxes, garlands and bows in the living room. "The truth is I never expected to have this much of the house ready for decorating this season.

"Ricky, your job is going to be to mark the price tags for these hand-painted nutcracker ornaments," she said, indicating the sheets of adhesive price stickers and the pen she'd set out on the pretty Victorian desk. "Then you can stick one on the back of each, okay?"

"Wow!" he said, picking up one and inspecting it more closely. "They have moving parts and no two are the same!"

"What's my job, Marina?" Molly asked, bouncing like a spring toy.

"First, you have to help me give this place a little atmosphere. Do you think you can reach that switch on the wall by that last tree?" she asked, pointing.

When Molly hopped and successfully flipped up the switch, every tree in the room lit with hundreds and hundreds of delicate white lights. The children clapped and cheered, and Marina had her reward for a morning's intensive labor getting each string placed to suit her.

"Now a little music," she said to Molly, handing her a cassette that advertised favorite children's Christmas songs that she'd found last week. She showed the child how to place it in the portable stereo she'd brought from the kitchen, and how to turn it on.

As "Jingle Bells" began playing, she pointed next to a mountain of artificial pine garland piled on one side of the room. "There's no putting this off any longer," she said, pretending to be overwhelmed by the prospect of their next task. "We have to get all that garland hung."

Molly gaped. "There must be miles of it!"

But as they set to work, she could tell the child felt very important about her responsibility. So did Ricky.

They began working on the railing first. Every few yards, Marina had Molly run over to the couch, where dozens of red velvet bows were neatly stacked, and they secured a bow to the garland. They finished just as Ricky completed his project.

Marina let them hang several of the ornaments on the first tree. She already had a three-foot-tall step-ladder for the higher spots, and supervised when they were on it. Then she had them carefully fill a garland-trimmed basket with wooden soldiers, and they placed it outside the railing for easy access by customers.

"What's next?" Molly said, her eyes glowing with pleasure.

"Well, maybe you should help me decide." Marina tapped her chin and pretended she couldn't make up her mind. "Should we put up these lovely silver bugles with the red ribbons from England, or those Scandinavian rocking horses?"

"Bugles!" Ricky shouted.

"Horsies!" Molly cried.

With a laugh, Marina said, "On second thought, maybe both will work." She pointed to the boxes of ornaments she'd already marked, and helped them start adding those to the tree.

"I hope you won't get so tired of this that you won't want to decorate your own tree," she told them, as she held the ladder for Ricky.

"No way," Ricky assured her. "Because last year all we had was a dinky one, and a dumb old wreath on the door."

"Yeah," Molly echoed mournfully. "No lights or nothin'."

Marina didn't know how to respond to that. She hadn't brought up the subject to remind them of unhappy moments or to snoop into their family life. But she found the revelation disheartening. Of course, she could understand Read's reason for disappointing the children; he could still have been mourning the loss of Gwenn, been tired, or perhaps needing to budget at that time. Did the children understand that?

"Let me ask you this," she began, carrying a basket to Molly for the ornaments she'd already labeled. "Did you enjoy being with your dad any less on Christmas morning?"

Molly looked as if she'd been asked if Santa Claus was really a fraud. "'Course not. Daddy's all we have."

"So then you had the most important part of the holiday."

"Guess so." Molly eyed her from beneath curling lashes. "But this is funner."

"Do you know that in European countries such as Holland, Germany and England they celebrate St. Nicholas Day, which is a few weeks earlier than our Christmas?"

"What do they do?" Molly asked, looking intrigued with the idea of another holiday.

"Children place their shoes by the fireplace, adding a carrot to them or a handful of hay for St. Nick's horse like we do cookies and milk for Santa Claus."

"And he leaves toys in their shoes?" the little girl asked, a bit confused. "They can't be very big ones."

"He brings sweets like *lebkuchen,* gingerbread and honey cakes. And fruit. You wouldn't think that's much, would you?"

Both children wrinkled their noses. Molly murmured, "I don't even know what most of that stuff is."

"The point is that for some poorer families, it's all the Christmas they have." She saw them ponder that thought.

"I guess you're saying that we don't have it so bad," Ricky murmured, his expression glum.

Marina didn't want him to think she didn't sympathize with their situation. "All I'm suggesting is that you'll be happier if you don't think of your life as being more or less than someone else's. Try to find joy in sharing moments with people you care about."

"Like this?"

"It depends. Are you having a good time?"

"Yeah."

"Then this is a little bit of Christmas. You see? We're making our own happiness. It's one of the best lessons I've learned in all the years I've spent traveling and watching other people and other cultures."

They worked, and chatted, and sang...and lost track of time. When the doorbell rang, Marina glanced out the window and saw it was close to dusk. That identified her caller.

"You wouldn't by any chance know where I can find two deserters about so big," he drawled, indicating the children's heights the moment she opened the door to him. "They used to live a few blocks from here, but I guess they've forgotten that."

With an apologetic smile, Marina invited him in. "It's my fault, Read. I know I should have sent them home half an hour ago, but..."

"I know. You were all having such a great time, you forgot to look out one of the dozens of windows in this place."

Sarcasm and all, he looked wonderful, like a lumberjack in the red plaid shirt and jeans that he wore beneath a heavy denim jacket. There were deeper fine lines around his eyes indicating fatigue, and his hair looked both windblown and hand mussed, but his rugged, masculine appeal affected her as strongly as ever.

Marina shut the door, aware of her heart pounding. "Did I make you stop in the middle of something important? Oh, dear... if I had my license already, I could have saved you the trip by driving them home."

He gave her a look that suggested she could have spared them the reminder of their failure there. "With what? You don't have a car, either." Muttering about children caring for children, he peered into the parlor. "So where are they?"

"In the living room. That was uncalled-for, Read. I'm not a child."

He paused, his gaze drifting over her black jumpsuit. "You're right, you're something far more dangerous—a beautiful, loving woman who lives in a fairy-tale house. Exactly how am I supposed to compete when you've enchanted my children?"

"You're their father. You don't have to."

With a skeptical look, he headed for the living room. Marina followed, thinking about what he'd said. His words would have been thrilling, except that he hadn't said them to compliment her. It didn't help that when they entered the room, she saw it as he must—that it was beginning to resemble the fairy tale he'd mentioned.

The children didn't notice them at first. Like merry elves they worked to adjust ornaments on a tree, their sweet smiles as bright as the lights framing them. About to tell them it was time to go, Marina felt Read's touch on her arm.

She turned to see him relax against the doorjamb, but it was his expression that made her breath catch in her throat. There was such a tenderness in him, a look of such hope for his children in his eyes. It made them radiate with warmth and softened a mouth that was usually hard, sensual but hard. In that instant, if she wasn't already in love with him, she would have fallen all over again.

"Have they been working like that all afternoon?" he asked, keeping his voice low.

"Yes. Why?"

"At home they usually bicker and tease."

Now that he'd mentioned it, she realized he was right; she hadn't heard them fuss or criticize each other the way she, too, had heard on occasion. It had her breaking into a smile. "It's the magic of the season taking its effect."

"It's some kind of magic," he murmured, shifting his gaze to her.

His move brought them close, so close Marina could see herself reflected in his eyes. His breath was warm on her face. Once they used to stand like this and talk of the wonder of finding each other, and what they could do to arrange for an hour more, thirty minutes, ten. It was heaven to experience it again.

"Lovely Marina." He lifted a hand to touch her cheek. "You're turning me inside out."

"Why fight this, *us,* so, Read?"

"Because somebody has to keep their head and be reasonable." As Marina began to protest, he moved his thumb to her lips. "No. Not tonight. Let's not argue. I want them to have this moment," he said, nodding to the children.

Just then Molly spotted him and shrieked. "Daddy! Look at what we did!"

Read caressed Marina's cheek one more time before he crossed the room, stooping just in time to catch his youngest as she launched herself at him. He lifted her high before settling her on his hip and hid a momentary rush of emotion by burying his face in the sweet warmth of her soft neck. She giggled and squirmed, but she smelled wonderfully of the bubble bath she'd used last night and something with butterscotch that Marina must have given them here. The brief communion helped take the edge off the loneliness that ate at him.

"What's the matter, Daddy? You feel sad."

Kids. They had better instincts than any adult he'd ever met. "Oh, yeah? So how does sad feel?"

"You're holding tighter and you stand real straight."

Despite the feeling that a boulder had lodged in his throat, Read growled, "The better to nibble some chicken neck, my dear," and playfully pretended he was doing just that. After listening to her squeal in delight for several seconds, he finally relented to her squirming attempts to break free and set her down. "Well, haven't you two been busy? When I first walked in here, I wasn't sure you weren't a couple of Santa's elves who'd lost their way from the North Pole."

"I priced all of those," Ricky said, pointing to his achievement.

"Bet your hand's sore." Proud, Read squeezed his son's shoulder. "I hardly recognize the room from the other day. You're all doing very well. You guys tired?"

"Not a bit. We could work another couple hours if Marina wants us to."

His son shot her a hopeful look. Read understood the adoration as much as the plea to intercede on their behalf.

"If I had my license and a car, I would happily drive you home to save your father another trip," she assured him, with an apologetic smile. "But as it is, I'm afraid you're out of luck."

At that moment the tape deck shut off and Read was left with Marina's words echoing in his ears. Guilt lashed at him sharply, and for good reason. He knew he'd pushed her into letting him give her lessons in the first place, and then used that opportunity to punish her for old hurts.

"How are the lessons going?" he asked with proper chagrin.

Marina grimaced. "I haven't had the time to call an agency and set up an appointment for lessons. Between taking care of things here, I've also started interviewing for sales help."

He knew she was busy, but doubted that was the only reason. "Are you sure you aren't feeling a little beat-up, too, because of what I did?" He supposed he deserved her stunned look. Hadn't he asked her only moments ago not to bring up anything that would upset the children?

Her gaze strayed to the children before flicking to him with confusion. "Read?"

"Let's try again."

"But you said... I don't want to—"

"I know. This is on my shoulders. Let's try again."

She didn't look convinced and seemed hesitant about his motives. Worse, his children were looking from him to her with increasing confusion and worry; they picked up on tension faster than he gave them credit. They deserved a break, too.

"You need that driver's license and I want to help. Consider it a thank-you for what you're doing for Ricky and Molly."

At least the children seemed to like that idea. Probably because they thought it meant even more access to Marina.

"You could teach both of us at the same time, Dad," Ricky declared. "It's not that long before I get my permit."

Read smiled. "Don't rush things."

"Well, if Ricky goes, can I?" Molly asked, tugging at her father's jeans.

Read touched his fingers to his lips to quiet them both. "Grown-ups talking here, okay?" Then he raised his gaze to Marina.

"I won't pretend to understand what you're doing," she told him at last.

He nodded. "I don't blame you, but I know this is fair and right. We could practice an hour right after I drop off the kids at school and day care."

"Aw," Ricky said, crossing his arms and pouting. "We want to come along."

"Not this time," Read replied, not taking his eyes off Marina. "Do we have a deal?"

"All right. I'll see you tomorrow."

The next morning he pulled into the driveway and found Marina waiting for him. She looked as if she had doubts about her decision—lovely and sophisticated in a royal blue jacket over a slim black dress, but hardly enthusiastic. Read gave her a wry smile as he climbed out and held the door for her to slip behind the steering wheel.

"Don't look as if you expect me to turn into a snarling bear if you blink."

"Give me a few minutes to convince myself that this isn't a figment of my imagination and I won't."

He nodded as he shut her door, then circled to the passenger side. "I deserve that," he said, settling beside her. Trying not to pay too much attention to her legs, he secured his seat belt. "You don't need to remind me that I've failed at finding a happy medium when it comes to dealing with people."

"I think we have that in common."

"You? You've always gotten along with everyone." Except him—and he was beginning to realize that was as much his fault as anyone's.

"As long as I kept to my role as obedient daughter and subordinate female."

That jarred him out of his silent brooding. "Who do you want to be?"

"I'm still trying to find out, that's the point. It's only been a few months since my father died and I declared my independence, Read. Don't you realize I'm like a freshly hatched egg?" Marina sighed as she explored the shape and strength of the steering wheel. "In Russia—at least the Russia my father knew and based all his judgments on—girls were raised by the seen-and-not-heard philosophy. I know that sounds archaic to you, but being demure was a refinement."

"But that's not who you are?" he asked, realizing they'd never talked in this depth before.

"I'm polite, not a doormat. I believe in manners."

"At the cost of speaking your mind?"

"Once... yes. When I was a minor. My father was legally responsible for me, and I lived in his house. Now I still believe respect is important, but for different reasons. And I accept that I'm responsible for my actions."

"I haven't shown you the good manners I should."

"No. But I understand why."

Read wondered if she really did. He shook his head. "Gwenn would never have tolerated what you have. As sunny-natured as she was, she didn't suffer fools for long."

"Read, you've succeeded in thoroughly confusing me. What am I supposed to say to something like that? What do you want from me?"

He wished he knew. Maybe he couldn't believe that they had a chance in hell of being happy due to their vastly different backgrounds and situations, but at least he could accept that what was in the past, his anger, was over and done with. It was time to move on.

His children adored her. She had already begun to enrich their lives, and it was clear they could only become better people for knowing her. He couldn't see himself remarrying in the foreseeable future, not even in the distant future—who was ever going to replace Marina in his heart? But maybe she could give to his children what he couldn't possibly accept for himself.

"Could we find some medium for friendship?" he asked with a humility he'd never thought himself capable of. "Let's get you that driver's license. You need it. I want to help you get it. Can that be enough?"

To his surprise Marina didn't reply, and instead started the truck's engine. Read watched her as she made a neat U-turn in her driveway, wondering what she was thinking. Several emotions played over her face, not the least of which were annoyance and disappointment. But he noticed determination, too—and something very feminine that worried him.

When she'd followed his brief direction and turned left out of the driveway, away from town, all without saying a word, he couldn't resist muttering, "Okay, out with it. What's going on in that busy little head of yours?"

"Tell me about Gwenn."

"Marina..."

"You said you wanted to be friends. Friends talk about their lives, their families."

Read groaned. She was going to do exactly what he wanted to avoid—talk about the past. But he'd set himself up for this by that stupid friendship line. "What do you want to know?"

"Where did you two meet?"

"She'd come into the store with her mother. Her mother knew my mother."

"Ah."

"What's that supposed to mean?"

"Mothers. They're a powerful ingredient in relationships. I often wonder if things would have turned out differently if my mother had been alive. So your mother and her mother arranged for you two to date?"

"This is America," he reminded her, though a little too defensively. "We asked each other."

"You came to this conclusion at the same time?" She shot him a quick look. "You mean like it was for us?"

"Eyes on the road." Read folded his arms across his chest, not at all pleased with this subject. He had no intention of telling her it wasn't anything *close* to the way it was with them, the lightning bolt of recognition and attraction. The almost feverish need to be in some physical contact, as if their very survival depended on it. The yearning and sweet, sweet passion... "She asked me out," he snapped, reluctantly admitting what would only complicate things. "I turned her down at first. It was only a few weeks after you left. I was blue and didn't want to see anyone, okay? My mother overheard and bullied me into giving her a call. The rest is history. Satisfied?"

"Zamichahtil'na."

"And what's that supposed to mean?"

"Quite remarkable. Out of that you had a son a short time later."

"A year, Marina. A little more than—and you were gone. *Gone.*"

She nodded slowly as if accepting that, but Read noticed she blinked a great deal, too. He prayed she wouldn't cry. He prayed harder that he wouldn't have to remind her about the stop sign ahead.

Braking, she came to a complete halt, looked both ways and then proceeded with caution. "I was in Paris the spring your son was born," she said quietly. "They say it's the city for lovers, but I stayed in my hotel room refusing to even look out a window, because the man I wanted as my lover, the only one I wanted, was an ocean away."

His teeth should have pulverized from the way he clenched them together. Maybe he deserved this, but he wished she would stop. "What good does it do to hurt me, Marina?" he asked when he couldn't keep quiet any longer. "I'm sorry, too. But life turned out differently."

"Yes. Very." She drove to where he'd directed her last time, to practice parallel parking. "I wonder if I could build up the courage to ask someone out."

He had to look out his passenger window so she wouldn't see him close his eyes against the pain. "You won't know until you try," he said without inflection. "Only one thing—don't practice on me."

He was grateful that he'd mentioned only an hour-long session, because after that Marina didn't speak to him again except to ask for directions, and the silence soon gave him a skull-numbing headache.

He couldn't complain about her driving, though. She proved to be the model of decorum—she kept to the speed limit, didn't miss a stop sign and *did* avoid every curb. Even so, on top of the headache, by the time they pulled into her driveway, his nerves were all wearing combat boots and stomping grapes in his stomach. Because she'd been suddenly turned into the robot she'd been for her father for so many years.

"That was good. Excellent," he told her, his palms damp. "You won't need more than a few hours before you'll be ready for your test." He envied her her shell of composure, but at the same time it troubled him. What would it take to shatter it?

"Thank you." She ran her hands around the steering wheel. "It felt good. Do you think I might be ready to buy myself a car for Christmas?"

Of all the things she might have brought up, that was the least expected. And it wasn't *by* Christmas, but *for*. Did that mean something deeper or was he reading too much into it? God, he couldn't bear it if he discovered she'd never received a Christmas gift in her life. But she had so many gorgeous clothes. On the other hand it would be just like her old man to dress her like a doll but never offer gifts from his heart. One thing he'd learned early on—Dmitri Davidov *owned* his daughter; he *loved* his music.

His throat raw, he managed, "If that's what you want. If you like, I could go with you to a dealership."

She nodded. "Yes, please. I wouldn't know if I was being taken advantage of or not. I promise I'll take up as little of your time as possible."

She was killing him. As she fumbled with her seat belt, Read brushed her hands away, released the catch and pulled her across the seat. When he saw the startled question in her eyes, he murmured, "Forgive me," and closed his lips over hers.

A soft sound rose from her throat. Was it protest or pleasure? He couldn't tell, and more important he didn't let it matter. He was too desperate to experience the pleasure of her, her warmth and vulnerability to him. And yet when she trembled at his deepening, searching kiss, then wrapped her arms around his neck, he could have wept with relief and gratitude for her acceptance. They had lost something precious. This was a blossom on the grave of what had been.

Murmuring her name, he coaxed her lips wider, drank in her soft sigh as greedily as he did the nectar from her lips and tongue. He showed her with his the dance he craved to experience with his entire body, but never would.

The kiss went on and on, bringing his body to a fever pitch and testing his endurance. By the time he forced himself to set her back on her side of the truck, Read had to swallow several times against an ache that was not only pounding in his throat but throughout his body.

"I should apologize for that," he said gruffly. "But it would be a lie."

"All right."

And to his amazement she smiled. It was a shaky smile, but he found it unsettling, nonetheless.

"What do you mean, 'all right'?"

"You're a fraud, Read," she murmured. "You care."

He considered trying to deny it, then felt even more shame. "It won't change what I've already told you," he muttered instead.

"If you say so." But she was all but beaming as she opened her door. "Do I get another lesson tomorrow?"

Not quite comfortable with the way she'd worded that, Read knew that even if he'd wanted to, he couldn't back down now. "Same time, unless you have something else planned?"

"I have an interview at eleven, but that won't interfere. I'll be ready."

Maybe *she* would be, Read thought as he watched her hurry up the front walkway, but he wasn't so sure about himself. Her words echoed in his mind, as sweetly taunting as the memory of her mouth, pliant and giving under his.

"Man, you are asking for trouble," he muttered as he made a three-point turn. "What's *wrong* with you?"

Chapter Seven

A cold front blew in earlier than expected the next day, bringing rain, and Read phoned to cancel Marina's driving lesson. She would have been depressed, except that he promised the children could still come later, guaranteeing that she would see him. What's more, despite his cautious tone, there had been a gruff tenderness in his voice.

Feeling more optimistic than she had in days, she held the interviews with prospective sales clerks as scheduled. The two ladies turned out to be such a delightful pair—sisters-in-law from a nearby retirement community, who were searching for something to do more than earning extra money—that Marina hired them on the spot. After convincing them to stay, she served tea and the baklava pastries from the recipe a Yugoslavian violinist's wife had shared with her on their last trip to the country before its political unrest.

The day passed so quickly, Mrs. Cotton and Mrs. Merriweather had barely left before Read dropped off the children. Expecting him to bring up the rear, she was stunned to see him turn and drive out.

"Why didn't your father come in?" she asked the two youngsters as they discarded their wet coats.

"He says he has a bunch of work he has to get back to," Molly offered, giving her a woman-to-woman look.

"I see." No doubt it was true, but Marina wondered how much of his avoidance was a reaction to what had happened yesterday. "Well, he's going to miss our fun, isn't he? Come on, today you two get to practice for St. Lucia's Day."

"What's that?" Ricky asked, rushing ahead to push open the swinging kitchen door.

"It's a Scandinavian holiday on the thirteenth of December when children get to do something special for their parents. Remember when I told you that the best part of holidays is the sharing? Well, this gives children a chance to contribute. And it has a lovely ceremony. I'll show you while we're getting our snack."

She told them about a guest house she stayed in once where Swedish children dressed in white for the event, and girls wore red sashes. "The eldest girl wore a wreath in her hair lit with candles, and after all the children prepared breakfast such as sweet cakes called *saffransbrod* and spicy cookies like *pepparkakor,* she led the processional delivering the treats and fresh coffee to their parents who were still sleeping."

"Oh, breakfast in bed!" Ricky said, automatically retrieving the milk for their hot chocolate. "Why didn't you say so? We do that for Dad on Father's Day."

"But we don't get to dress up," Molly said, fingering a curl. She corkscrewed it around and around her finger. "Since I'm the only girl, would I get to wear the wreath, Marina?"

"That's the way I understand the tradition works."

The children decided they might like to try that celebration. But they agreed that their father would get pretty nervous if they tried to make anything more complicated than tuna on white bread or cereal. After promising to bake them something here and letting them hide it at their house, she led them to the parlor to start work on the Advent wreath displays.

They'd been working for only a short while when, as predicted, the rain changed to sleet. Ricky noticed first and his shout drew them all to the window.

"First snow! First snow!" Molly cried, climbing up on the windowsill.

"Maybe," Ricky murmured, looking hopefully at the sky.

Marina hoped it would change, too. She didn't want to think of Read or anyone else having to travel in this dangerous slush. She almost didn't believe her eyes when his truck turned into the driveway.

Squeals of pleasure from Molly and groans from Ricky had her shushing them and urging them to the front door. As Molly ran before them, Marina put her arm around Read's son.

"What's the matter?"

"He'll make us go home. We're only getting started."

"You can't blame him for worrying."

"But we're fine here. Why can't we stay?"

Marina had an idea, but she couldn't share it. Not in good conscience. "Let's wait and see what he has to say."

He slipped and glided down the sidewalk, winning giggles from his daughter. Molly hugged him the instant he finished stomping his boots on the doormat and crossed the threshold.

"Daddy! Did you come to work, too?"

"A little. I also came to deliver something. Here."

With a sheepish smile, he brought out a wooden sign from under the cover of his jacket. Marina stared at the elegant lettering that read *The Christmas House*.

"It has two sides, so you can hang it out front where traffic will be able to read it as they come from either direction. Of course, I haven't put a finish on it yet. I thought you might want to choose that yourself. And I'll put hooks down at the bottom here, too, in case you want me to make another sign listing your hours." As if suddenly realizing he was rambling, he clammed up.

"Read...I don't believe it," she murmured, reaching out to touch the scrolled borders. "This is fantastic! And perfect!"

Although the children raved, too, he didn't seem convinced. "It's probably not as fancy as what you had in mind...."

"Read, with all the many things there are to remember, the thought of a sign had slipped my mind completely." She took the gift from him and held it up, laughing with delight. "It's the most marvelous thing. My business has a sign!"

"It's much better than the one you made for yourself," Ricky assured him. "That one only says No Credit—Beware of Dog."

Marina looked from father to son. "I didn't know you have a dog."

"We have Raspberry," Ricky said, a doleful expression lengthening his face.

Read cleared his throat. "Raspberry sleeps a great deal. Raspberry ran away from his previous home because he wanted owners who understand he likes to sleep. Not go for walks. Not play ball or fetch the stick. Sleep."

"I see." Marina fought back a grin. "No wonder I didn't see him when I came to your house that day. And how did he get his name?"

Both Read and Ricky pointed to Molly. But it was Ricky who said, "When we got him, almost every name we suggested she couldn't pronounce without sputtering raspberries, so Dad said we might as well call him that."

Clearly delighted with her part in history, Molly hugged her father's leg and giggled. "Go hang up the sign, Daddy!"

"It's not ready to be hung yet, sweetie." He tapped the tip of her nose and winked at her before wrapping his arm around Ricky's shoulders. "So how are things going here?"

"Fine. We're *really* busy working on Advent wreaths," Molly declared, before her brother could answer. "You know what they are, Daddy?"

"No, sugarplum, I guess I don't."

"It's a wreath like the one we had on the door last Christmas, only it starts out plain, you know? We're going to have small ones and bigger ones, so people can choose, and then we'll have all these different things to decorate them. You have to have candles, too. Then you hang the wreath from the light or put it on the table, and you sing and eat."

"My," Read murmured, using one ringlet to tickle her upturned face. "You're just a bubbly brook of information these days."

"Marina told us the story," Ricky interjected quickly. "Advent starts right after Thanksgiving and you light one candle each Sunday until Christmas. Can we do that, Dad?"

When Marina felt Read's gaze shift to her, she offered an apologetic smile. "They tend to remember the festivities more than the meaning behind them, but they *are* learning, Read."

Before he could respond, Molly tugged at his hand. "Marina said we could choose a wreath each and decorate it the way we wanted as part of our pay."

"Uh-oh," he drawled. "There go the profits."

"What you really should know," Marina told him, enjoying this gentle side of him, "is that some people spread the celebration over thirty-seven days."

"Thirty-seven candles? Does this thing come with a fire extinguisher?"

She laughed. "Don't worry, I'm recommending they keep it down to the four, and they're promising they'll only light their candles when you're there with them."

"Thanks. I think."

Marina turned to the youngsters. "Why don't you get back to unwrapping those Advent animals and set them on the middle shelf, okay?"

As they charged to the parlor, Read lifted an eyebrow. "Animals?"

"It's the Peaceable Kingdom theme." She hugged her sign to her heart. "Why don't you take off your jacket and join us?"

"Well, I was going to go back to the house. I need to work a bit more. I just thought with this weather..."

"Oh, Read. The children did want to stay a bit longer." She let her eyes telegraph even more appeal.

"It wouldn't be smart to attempt this trip again." He tilted his head toward the outdoors. "I have a feeling in a few hours that mess is going to freeze solid."

"I understand. You're right, of course."

"That also means we'll have to skip another practice tomorrow."

"I've waited this long for my license, what's a few more days?"

It was a rhetorical question that she didn't expect to get answered, but it also left her with nothing more to say. Since he didn't add anything, either, they spent the next several seconds listening to the children chattering away in the next room.

"Uh..." Read abruptly indicated the sign.

"Oh, yes." Marina handed it over. "Read, thank you again. It's wonderful."

"Did you think of a shade you'd prefer?"

"Why don't you choose? You've done such a beautiful job already."

He seemed pleased with that. But a moment later Marina realized he wasn't going to comment on his ideas—or anything else. Silence stretched again.

"Would you like a cup of tea? Coffee?"

He simply shook his head, his gaze resting longer and longer on her.

Marina felt a warm rush sweeping through her. "Read?"

"Hmm?"

"You're staring."

"Sorry."

He turned away and started for the door. About to reach for the knob, Marina followed and touched his arm. He froze and stared at her hand.

"I'll get a shovel from the truck and clean your sidewalk."

"I like when you stare."

"The problem is that I want to do more than stare."

"Then why don't you?"

"The children..."

"Are busy enjoying themselves. They're not paying any attention to us." When he didn't make any comment to that, she wondered what she needed to do to reach him. On impulse she stepped between him and the door and studied him sadly. "Was Gwenn experienced when you met her? Is that it? Don't I have her... appeal?"

"Marina."

"You're right. That was unfair. But she was beautiful, yes?"

"She looked like Molly," he admitted, growing more tense. "She had a kind of perkiness, a cuteness that was..."

"Sexy."

"*Yes,*" he whispered angrily. Dropping the sign on the chair beside them, he boxed her against the door with his hands. "But you're wrong if you think there's only one kind of sexiness."

"What other kind is there?"

"You know damned well. The kind you have, romantic...exotic...untapped...sweet."

"How can sweet be sexy?"

"You tell me," he said, and fastened his mouth to hers.

His self-control had lasted barely more than twenty-four hours, but Read ignored his sense of failure for the sheer pleasure of touching Marina again. God, she was kitten soft, and the cuddly pink tunic she was wearing only made her softer. How could one innocent woman bring him to this state? He was at the point where he ached through and through when he wasn't near her, and he ached even worse when she tempted him like this.

Her lips parted for him and he greedily took what she offered, then asked for more. No matter what happened, he would never kiss another woman without wanting Marina. The truth seared through his body like the hottest of flames. When she slipped her hands into his jacket to wrap her arms around his waist, he groaned softly and used his body to pin her more firmly against the door. If he could imprint himself on her...if he could, she would be his forever.

And yet he knew restraint. She was so willowy and slight compared to him. He could keep her his prisoner with one hand, but behind his closed lids he imagined using both to explore her. Once he had, and he could still remember every exquisite curve and hollow of her body. She'd trembled with excitement and nervousness, but heaven love her, she'd trusted him so. She did now, but he knew she shouldn't.

Aware he was fast approaching an edge, he dragged his mouth from hers and buried his face in her hair. "You have to let me get out of here. Now."

"I know." But she didn't remove her hands from around his waist.

"The kids will be getting curious if you don't get back in there soon."

"You're right."

She did begin to let go then, but slowly, and first she eased her hands along his sides and ran them over the expanse of his chest. He knew she could feel the tautness of his muscles and the heavy pounding of his heart, caused as much by her provocative touch as the expression of admiration and wonder on her face. She was playing with fire, and even if she didn't know what power she had over him, he did.

With a hoarse whisper of her name, he took hold of her hand and lifted it to his mouth for a brief but passionate kiss, then he swept her up and out of his way. "Go to the children."

"Stay with us. I'll make us dinner."

"I can't. As soon as I get the walk cleared, we need to leave."

"I won't ask you to kiss me again."

That was rich. "You didn't ask me this time."

"You just didn't hear the words...just as you can't take what's already yours."

Heaven help him. "No, sweetheart. That's where your logic hits a giant pothole. I may have been the first guy to make your heart race, but I'm the last one you should set your dreams on. Too many miles on this model, and a heavy mortgage for good measure. I'm nowhere near your class, and the sooner you accept that fact, the less painful this is going to be for all of us."

Her shattered expression was nearly his undoing.

"Look," he said urgently, reaching out to grasp her by her upper arms. "I don't want to hurt you. I don't want to hurt any of us. So help me. *Help me, Marina.*"

Marina didn't regret having been so honest with Read. She was in love with him. It was inconceivable to try to fall out of love with him. Nor did she agree with his theory about why they couldn't be happy together. But witnessing his anguish touched her deeply.

After a night and a day of soul-searching, while the heavens bestowed them with several inches of sleet followed by a few more of snow, she came to the conclusion that she did not want to become someone he worked to avoid. In addition, she couldn't bear thinking of being denied visits with Molly and Ricky. If she was such a torment to him, then she would help him as he'd asked. Maybe if she became this untouchable creature he thought he could deal with, he would see what an impossible lie that was, too.

At least with the improving weather, her life became busier, and that gave her little time to feel sorry for herself. More stock arrived every day, and she had additional meetings with Mrs. Cotton and Mrs. Merriweather to get them familiar with the house and inventory. Then there were permits to obtain, an accountant to hire and advertising to arrange.

Between the weather and those business commitments she only managed to work in one driving lesson during the week, during which time Read never mentioned their last meeting. It was the only dark cloud and moment of awkwardness in what otherwise proved a satisfying day. Less thrilling was that she saw the children only twice because of her conflicting schedule and Molly catching a cold.

Before she knew it, Thanksgiving loomed. She notified Read that she was ready to open at least the front rooms of The Christmas House—if he could finish putting in the front checkout counter in time. He promised it would be ready Friday. On Thursday evening, excited about seeing Read again, as well as getting this last hurdle to opening out of the way, a disturbing cloud from the past shadowed her anticipation when she received a call from Vladimir Lesko, her father's manager.

On Thursday morning when the doorbell rang, she hurried downstairs, hoping it was Read, hoping they would have a chance to talk. Instead she opened the door to find a tall, elegantly dressed man with unapologetically flirtatious gray eyes and a lazy smile.

"Marina Davidov? I'm Jeremy Cameron. Did Vlad call you about me?"

He had indeed. That was why she'd reached into her closet for one of her more businesslike, mature outfits. She'd chosen a sophisticated cranberry suit with a slim skirt and little gold chains linking the matching gold buttons that she hoped gave her an image of confidence as well as independence.

"Yes." She stepped back to allow the blond-haired man into her home. "But I wish he had given me a bit more warning that you were coming. As you can see, I'm not exactly prepared for guests."

"My fault," he assured her suavely, as he took her hand. "When I get these brainstorms there's no point in trying to stop me. I'm afraid I was quite prepared to do whatever necessary to wear down old Vladimir if he resisted my offer."

"If you knew him better, you would realize that Vladimir never passes up any opportunity to promote my father." Marina withdrew her hand.

"Aha . . . so you're the hard sell."

"Guilty."

"Delightful," he murmured, his smile deepening.

She indicated his chesterfield overcoat. "If I can take that for you, we'll go to my father's workroom. I'm expecting a—the carpenter to finish in here momentarily, and it's bound to get noisy."

"You're redecorating?" he asked, doing an intensive survey as he put down his leather portfolio and slipped out of his coat.

"In a manner of speaking. I'm turning the house into a specialty shop."

"Charming. I've always admired the entrepreneurial spirit. No doubt your father would be filled with pride."

"He would hate the idea," Marina told him, more than a little amused at his ingratiating demeanor even as she admired his finely tailored gray suit. "So does Vladimir, since I broke the news to him yesterday. He believes I should become a living memorial to my father—and that brings us to why you're here. Why don't we go this way . . ." She folded his coat over her arm and led the way to her father's room.

She'd prepared tea, being told that Jeremy Cameron was part English and had finished his education at Oxford. While he took a casual tour of the room, admiring awards, photographs and various memorabilia her father had enjoyed surrounding himself with, Marina prepared his tea English-style for him and Russian-style for herself. She also discreetly studied him, and found him attractive in a polished, cultured way, exactly the type of man her father would approve of, which automatically made her wary.

"This is marvelous," the man said, finally joining her on the couch that faced the piano. "This would be a perfect backdrop for what I had planned."

Over the next few minutes, Marina listened to a summary of Jeremy Cameron's proposal. It was exactly what Vladimir had aspired for her during the reception after her father's funeral. She had turned him down—far too politely, considering his timing—and her instinctive reaction now was one of rejection, as well. Not because it wasn't a good idea; her father deserved the immortalization he would undoubtedly receive. But she had given twenty-eight years to Dmitri Davidov. Who would condemn her for taking some time for herself?

About to tell him so, she heard a sound at the front door. Certain it was Read, Marina excused herself and went to let him in.

Although his eyes reflected deep admiration at her appearance, Read had obviously noticed the strange car in the driveway. It had a pronounced effect on his demeanor.

"I'm coming at a bad time?"

"No, it's all right. Someone is here from Boston. My father's longtime friend and manager, who I've asked to continue overseeing Father's estate, sanctioned an idea and Mr. Cameron is here to explain it to me."

His gaze was sweeping and concerned. "You don't look happy."

"It's just that I thought I wouldn't have to face this so soon."

"Would you like me to come back later?"

"Read, I need that counter." She was about to say more, but she heard footsteps behind her. At the same time she saw Read tense.

She turned. "Jeremy."

"Excuse me if I'm intruding," her guest drawled, glancing from her to Read, "but is there some way I can be of assistance?"

His inspection of Read's work clothes clearly stated that he'd already categorized and rejected him as having limited importance. Marina had only one reaction to that.

"Jeremy Cameron, this is Read Archer, a longtime friend and the craftsman behind the displays for The Christmas House."

To his credit Jeremy recognized his gaffe and recovered quickly. "Archer. Nice work."

Read shook his hand, but offered no response until he refocused on her. "I think I should come back in an hour or two."

"Really, that won't be necessary." She did not want him to leave her. Maybe handling Jeremy Cameron was her responsibility, but just knowing Read was in the house gave her strength.

For a moment he looked as if he might argue. "All right. I'll be as quiet as I can," he said almost gently. "But if I do intrude, you tell me, promise?"

"If she doesn't, I will," Jeremy said, easing his arm around Marina and directing her toward the study. "She has such a soft voice, I'll resent missing a word of what she says."

Marina could only mouth a thank-you at Read before Jeremy closed the doors behind them. However, if she was a little miffed at the television producer's take-charge attitude, she couldn't deny that he was skillful at making amends and could be lethally charming.

"Before you scold me," he told her, holding up a hand and placing another over his heart, "let me state in my defense that I have an irrepressible tendency to protect the fairer sex—I know it's an outdated exercise, but there you are. In fact I have an elderly aunt back in Boston who insists I should be frozen until such time that science figures out what to do with a dinosaur like me. Would you believe she whacks me with her cane whenever I pass through her threshold, simply because she knows I'll upset her with my chivalrous nature before leaving? By the way, she collects fine crystal, and you have an angel in the foyer that I'd love to purchase for her."

It was one of the most expensive items she carried, and she had a feeling he'd recognized that on sight. "Your aunt sounds like a wise lady who's not only fortunate to have a clever nephew, but a generous one."

His grin reflected unabashed pleasure. "I have a feeling she would love you. Maybe I can woo her out here to meet you sometime?"

As they took their seats again, Marina found she was able to smile again. "Please do."

"It's a promise. Now, as for my proposal..."

They talked for almost an hour more. Jeremy gave her several reports and outlines to back up what he had in mind, and a tentative schedule. Marina grabbed on to it as her chief excuse.

"This would be in direct conflict with my own plans for the grand opening of my business," she said, scanning the three-page filming schedule.

"Nothing there is written in stone," he assured her. "We'll work it out. What's not negotiable about the contract is *you*. We must have you or it won't be the same. Look at you—you have the face, the presence. The man's passion speaks through those exotic eyes of yours."

He was very gallant when she walked him out, his portfolio and gift-wrapped angel under one arm. He bowed over her hand and raised it to his lips. "Take your time if you must," he murmured, "but understand that I won't take no for an answer."

When she shut the door, Marina turned to see Read straightening from behind the new counter. She could tell by his set expression that he hadn't missed anything.

"The counter's going to be wonderful."

"Thanks. How did the meeting go?"

She lifted one shoulder. "He wants me to host a lecture series on my father's work for public and cable television."

Read whistled softly. "Congratulations."

"I turned him down."

"Good grief—why?"

She couldn't believe he needed to ask her that. "Haven't you been listening to a word I've been saying all this time? I want to have my life. Mine. Why does everyone constantly insist that I be fed intravenously through his life! *Yes*, I knew him best. But no one is interested in knowing that dark, paranoid and selfish person. They want to hear about the genius who filled concert halls for over forty years and made grown men weep and generations dream with his music. They want to believe that art is a gift without consequence."

"I didn't mean to upset you."

"No one means to upset me, Read. But no one is interested in hearing about reality, either." Marina laughed, feeling a little paranoid herself. "All I'm trying to do is find my own worth for being on this planet. I loved my father better than anyone ever will because I understood him. He was brilliant. A blazing star the likes of which we'll never see again. But before I help his public give him his proper place in history, I need to secure my own."

Chapter Eight

Marina eyed the tray of gingerbread men on the front counter and wondered if she shouldn't carry them back to the kitchen and wrap them as Mrs. Merriweather had first suggested before they dried out much more. It was the Monday before Thanksgiving and nearly noon, but so far they'd only had a trickle of customers.

"Don't worry, dear," Mrs. Merriweather cooed, looking up from where she sat behind the counter knitting in a rattan rocking chair. "Everyone's thinking about turkey dinner and trying to remember to put cranberry sauce on their shopping lists. This town is no different than anywhere else. We don't get serious about Christmas shopping until the last of the turkey has been baked in a casserole."

"I'm sure you're right." But it was difficult not to feel a little anxious. She'd already spent as much as she'd budgeted for this month on advertising, and between renovations and inventory, she'd dipped into her savings as much as she thought wise. If she'd been wrong about the store, she would still be fine. But she didn't want to live off her inheritance, she wanted to add to it for the sake of the family she hoped someday to have.

"Look, here comes a car now," Mrs. Merriweather cried, pointing to the window. "Oh, and another is following it in. See? I told you. Once folks see that open sign out there, curiosity will do the rest."

Marina was glad she'd told Read to go with that simple word and not spend time on hours that might change later. "I'll go and turn on the music again, and tell Mrs. Cotton she can switch on the display of motion Santas," Marina replied, already heading for the living room.

For the next few hours, Marina was kept busy greeting customers, supervising her new employees and answering numerous questions. It was true that there seemed to be a great number of curious people wandering in who were as interested at having a peek at her as they were at browsing through her displays. And while a number of them picked up an ornament or small figurine, no one purchased any of the more elaborate and costly items. It wasn't long before the cash register reflected that.

Her only bright moment came later in the afternoon when Read arrived with Molly and Ricky. "What a nice surprise," she said, bending to catch Molly as she ran into her arms. "I didn't expect to see you today."

"Did you think we wouldn't be here to help celebrate your first day?" Read asked, as she accepted a
hug from Ricky, too. "Besides, I told the kids they
could each pick an ornament for the tree. We always
put it up right after Thanksgiving dinner."

The mention of the holiday was another reminder
of disappointment. She'd thought, hoped, that by now
Read would have invited her to join them, but so far
he hadn't said a word. The sisters-in-law, Cotton and
Merriweather, did, and there'd been a few other more
formal invitations, including one from Jeremy Cameron, but as thoughtful and generous as they were,
they simply didn't hold the weight an invitation from
Read would have.

"That's a wonderful tradition," she told the children, hanging their coats on the employee coatrack.
"Well, to start off right, have one of our gingerbread
men. Then you need to go in the back and see the
newest ornaments from Czechoslovakia. They're
mouth-blown and painted. Molly, there's a pink heart
I think you'd love, and Ricky, wait until you see the
pecan-shell reindeer a local craftsman made. Come
on, I'll show you."

They stayed for an hour—long enough to cheer her
up and help the rest of the day pass. She didn't even
let herself get depressed when they left and Read still
hadn't mentioned more about Thanksgiving.

On Tuesday she used the quiet time to straighten up,
do the bookkeeping and bake a bit. She also took
courage from Mrs. Cotton and Mrs. Merriweather and
relented when they suggested they break early for them
to take her for her driver's-license test. They reasoned
that if they could negotiate a vehicle through Berry-

field at their age, surely she had learned enough to do the same.

Less than an hour later she was a legal Massachusetts driver.

To celebrate, the ladies treated her to apple cider and a fresh-baked chocolate-chip cookie at a fresh produce market, and by the time she returned home she was surprisingly exhausted. She turned in early, confident that tomorrow just had to be even better.

By Wednesday Read was tired of being noble, and at least for the moment he talked himself out of every good reason to keep his kids separated from Marina. Even though he'd only begun the armoire for the foyer and had nothing to deliver, he surprised his son and daughter by picking them up after Ricky got out of school and driving over to her place. He had no idea of the excuse he would use to explain their presence, but no sooner did they arrive than it no longer mattered.

They found Marina in the parlor with a tall, elegantly dressed woman who stood stiffly glaring at her. On the floor was a shattered figurine, the largest crystal angel in her beloved display.

"Well, it's your own fault for not having them out of reach of children," the woman declared. "My Teddy never does anything like this at home."

There was a decided strain around Marina's small mouth. "Excuse me, but he intentionally knocked the item off the table. This was after you told him that it was time to leave."

"I see, so now you're not only calling me a liar, but you're suggesting I should pay for that?" The woman grabbed her freckle-faced child's hand. "I certainly will not. Come, Teddy. I have no intention of spending another minute in this—place. There's nothing here Mommy could possibly want."

Despite having come in at the end of the scene, Read was so angry he wanted to shake the woman until her scrawny neck snapped. Beside him Molly bit back a child's moan of despair at the shattered figurine. Belatedly he recognized it as one she'd spoken of so often, ever since Marina had first unpacked it. He drew her against him and patted her back consolingly, protecting her from the glare he bestowed on the rude woman as she stalked past him out the door with her smiling son in tow.

However, it was Marina who had the bulk of his attention. When the door slammed behind the woman, Marina clapped a hand to her mouth, but there was no holding back the tears that flooded her eyes and poured down her cheeks. Knowing she wouldn't want the children to see her so upset, he touched Ricky's shoulder. "You know what? I think some of those glass icicles would look pretty good on our tree. Why don't you take your sister and go see if there are any left."

Exchanging wise glances with him, Ricky nodded. "Sure, Dad. C'mon, Molly. Dad needs to talk to Marina."

"But I want to hug her. She's crying."

"Later. Come *on.*"

Without waiting for his son to coax his daughter from the room, Read went to Marina, carefully led her away from the glass and drew her into his arms. It was exactly what he would have avoided doing under different circumstances, but he knew it was precisely what she needed at the moment.

"How can people be so mean?" she asked, her voice raw from repressed sobs.

"It's an acquired talent."

"D-don't make jokes, Read. He broke the most b-beautiful angel."

He hugged her more closely to him. "I know, sweetheart. I'm sorry. I was only trying to— Heck. I suppose there isn't any way to soften the hurt when something like this happens. I'm just sorry it had to happen to you."

"It had been such a nice day so far. Quiet, so I told Mrs. Cotton and Mrs. Merriweather to wait until Friday's grand opening before they came back in, but there had been a few customers who made nice purchases. Then this horrible woman and her monstrous little boy—"

"Try to put it behind you." Repeatedly, soothingly, he stroked her back. "Maybe this is the worst of it and it will be nothing but good moments from here on out."

"No, it's a sign. I was a fool to think I could make this work. Naive."

"You forgot to add incompetent."

"And stupid."

"Stop it!" Read took firm hold of her upper arms and gave her just enough of a shake to force her to meet his gaze. "You've worked too hard to let one arrogant woman ruin your dreams for you."

"But look—" awkward though it was, she gestured to indicate the empty place "—no one's coming, and that shattered glass represents more than I made all day!"

"It'll get better. Give people time. Grand opening isn't until Friday, and that's the official start of the Christmas shopping season, as all the experts say."

"What difference does that make if no one comes *here?*"

He could have laughed at the nonsensical approach to her logic, but knowing how badly that would hurt, he sighed instead, and before he could stop himself let impulse reign. "You know what you need? You need to get your mind off all this. Have Thanksgiving dinner with us."

She'd barely had a chance to react when he heard a commotion behind him.

"Yeah!"

Before he could see how his kids had managed to eavesdrop on their conversation, they were attacked from behind. Read was forced to release Marina just in time to keep himself from being impaled by icicles.

"Whoa." He eased those from their grasp, leaving them free to swarm her with hugs and pleas.

"It would be so much *fun,*" Molly gushed, her sweet face adoring. "You could come early and feed the birdies, and meet Raspberry while he's 'wake and everything!"

"Dad never remembers how to make the stuffing," Ricky added. "You could help him do that."

"Tell her 'bout the dishes," Molly whispered loudly to her brother.

"Oh, yeah—and on Thanksgiving we use paper plates so nobody has to miss the game because of dirty dishes."

Read covered his face with his hands and rubbed hard. He figured that if he did it long enough he would wake up and this would all be a bad dream. Who needed the threat of famine and crime when he had his own personal town criers to spread good news around?

"Don't forget about setting the table," he added drolly.

Molly brightened. "Oh, yeah—you could help do that, too!"

With a deep sigh, Read took his chances and faced Marina. "Now you know the way *not* to coax someone to come to dinner."

"It's a wonderful way," Marina insisted.

And it seemed she meant it, because she was laughing instead of crying, and brushing the remaining tears from her cheeks. Read thought that after witnessing Ricky and Molly being born, she was the prettiest sight he'd ever seen.

"Well, what can I do beforehand?" she asked everyone. "What can I bring?"

Read quickly placed a hand over both of his kids' mouths. "Just yourself."

"Then you'll have to take those icicles as my gift to you."

He tried to protest, but she remained adamant, asking only what time she should be there. "Uh..." He had no idea what to tell her. He'd never invited anyone to dinner before. "Tell us what's a good time for you and we'll pick you up."

"Well...oh! I almost forgot—I have the most marvelous news to tell you! I have my license!"

She quickly told them her story about her two senior-citizen employees taking her out yesterday on a lark. At first Read felt a bit cheated, but the more she told them, the brighter her mood became, and the happier he felt for her.

"Then you need a car!"

Whoever said it first, they all ended up agreeing. Read convinced Marina that whether she settled on something that day or not, she needed to take the first step.

Whether it was the situation with her last customer or a growing confidence in herself, Marina surprised him by agreeing. She even insisted on leaving the mess to clean up later, and snatched up her coat and purse to follow them out the door.

"Now, the best way to do this is not to get your hopes up, and don't feel pressured," he told her as they pulled into the dealer's lot a few minutes later.

But to his amazement, an hour later they were exiting the dealership and she was the proud new owner of a sleek white sedan. To Read it looked part space rocket, part shark, and the kind of vehicle that when wrapped around her would turn heads at every stoplight.

"Are you sure about the color?" he'd asked, when she'd first picked it. He thought of all the reasons it would be problematic, like how it got dirty fast and how it would be darned near invisible in fog.

"White is a good color for starting over," she'd replied with a slow, firm nod of her head.

He stopped worrying about her after that. He even managed to keep a smile on his face when she wrote out a check to the salesman for the whole amount of the car. Never mind that he would have asked for what terms the finance company was offering these days, and if they accepted mouthy but healthy kids as collateral.

"Sorry you can't get it until Friday," he told her now, as he started back to her house.

"Me, too." Her laugh reflected her pleasure, and that she was feeling a little dazed about the whole thing, too. "I never thought I'd be anxious for a holiday to be over before, but—" She cast him a mortified look. "Oh, I didn't mean that the way it sounded."

He waved away her apology. "Believe me, I know what you're feeling. My first car was a lemon with four previous owners, and I had to work a second job for six months to afford it. But I didn't sleep the night before my father took me to town to pick it up."

"Can we go with you when you get your new car, Marina?" Molly asked from the back seat.

"I hope so—and I hope your father will let you two ride with me back to the house." But while they cheered in the back seat, Marina focused on him. "I was thinking, though...about tomorrow? Don't worry about picking me up. You'll have enough to do as it is. Just tell me what time you usually eat, and I'll be there."

Read wanted to argue about that, but she would hear none of it. Her timing was good, too. It was difficult to manage a shrug when he was turning into her driveway. "Well, as for time..."

"We usually eat before one game and after another," Ricky offered when he hesitated.

"Game?"

Ricky gasped. "The football games. All the best College Bowl games are on Thanksgiving Day! Haven't you ever watched them before?"

After releasing her seat belt, Marina turned in her seat and shook her head, giving him a very apologetic look. "Sorry. Is that a terrible confession?"

"Yes!" the boy replied.

"No!" Molly declared, leaning forward. "You come early, though, and you can watch the parade with me."

Read liked that idea. "Come when you can, okay?"

The next morning he started glancing out the window for her at eight, willing her to come. By nine he was wondering if he shouldn't call to see if she was all right, if she'd had a change of heart, and would she please let him come pick her up, so he would stop trying to give himself whiplash every time a car drove down the street. At ten a taxi pulled up before the house and the only reason no one heard his great sigh of relief was that the kids were screaming with excitement and charging for the front door.

She looked like a snow queen . . . a princess at the least. Beneath the coat Ricky helped her remove, she wore a winter white knit dress with seed pearls stitched around a yoke collar and teardrop earrings with matching pearls. There were even seed pearls in the combs holding back the heavy fall of her hair from her face. She looked regal and pure—and she left him with the strongest compulsion to go wash his hands again.

Molly was enraptured, too, and took her immediate attention by asking to touch the combs. After hanging up the coat, Ricky used the time to tuck in his dress shirt, which Read had been asking him to do for the past two-plus hours. But Marina didn't let them hover and flatter for too long. She'd brought gifts.

"I'm glad you like the combs, Molly, because these are for you," she said, reaching into a shopping sack and bringing out a prettily wrapped tissue-paper parcel. "And the earrings were mine when I was a little girl. You have to promise me that you'll save them for special occasions like this.

"And Ricky," she continued, "this shirt is for you. The man at the store assured me that most of the boys who come in there are fans of this team."

Both of the children were thrilled with their presents, and Read was pleased that he didn't have to remind them to say thank you. As they hugged her, however, he did gently scold. "You weren't supposed to do that, and when did you have time?"

"I was so excited after you dropped me off last night, I phoned for a cab and went out again." She reached into her bag once more and came out with a bottle of wine and another of brandy. "I wasn't quite sure what to bring you."

Read didn't know much about wine, but he whistled at the brandy. "Now you're making me feel terrible. I didn't—"

"You've invited me to be a part of you and your family's celebration," she interjected, bringing out the last item—a bouquet of white flowers. "That means the world to me. Now show me where I can find something to put these in or we're going to have a very wilted centerpiece."

They all directed her to the kitchen. While Read hunted for something that bore a close similarity to a vase, Molly and Ricky tried to introduce Marina to Raspberry. The overweight rusty brown mongrel lay on his side under the kitchen table, and no amount of coaxing succeeded in getting him to do more than lifting one eyelid and giving a single lazy thump of his tail.

"Why do I get the feeling he's waiting for lunch?" Marina asked, joining Read at the sink.

He turned on the tap to start filling the tallest drinking glass he could find. Behind him the kids kept picking up Raspberry's paw and trying to coax him into shaking hands.

"Because you're right. That mutt only knows two locations to move to—under there, and the back stoop where he can soak up the most sunshine. The only time he barks is when someone gets too close to his food bowl." But as he set the glass on the counter so she could begin work, he couldn't resist adding, "You do look lovely." He knew he'd been the one to insist they not get personal again, but denying the words would have been a greater offense.

For an instant her eyes grew soft. Yearning. Then she forced a big smile and theatrically bowed. "Thank you, kind sir. I'm not too early, am I?"

No, he was ten years too late in realizing that dreams were only dreams, and that he'd been damned lucky to have her for the short time he did. He would be even more lucky if she would let him be her friend. He would be the best friend she could ever have. "Nope," he said, matching her smile. "You're perfect."

Once the flowers were arranged and on the table, Read insisted that Marina join the kids in the living room. "Just enjoy yourself for a while. I'll be with you as soon as I finish stuffing the bird and shoving it in the oven."

Preparations were a little more complicated than that—there were the potatoes to be peeled and cooked, and the vegetables to be readied for warming—but he'd done most everything else earlier, so he didn't take too long. When he joined them, his kids were entertaining Marina with stories about holidays past.

"My first parade I ate all snacks and got stuffed," Molly informed her, as if reciting a scholastic achievement. "I got such a tummy ache, I didn't even eat no dinner for a week, right, Daddy?"

"Well...not quite, but you were one sick puppy."

Marina lifted his daughter onto her lap and adjusted the child's combs. "I'm so sorry to hear that."

"That's okay. Daddy didn't know nuthin' 'bout cooking that year. I 'member 'cause Mommy went to heaven only a little before."

Marina bit her lip and hugged the child. "I'm very glad to be sharing this Thanksgiving with you, Molly. All of you."

By the time they sat down to dinner, Read had already realized that just like in the old days—and contrary to her privileged background—Marina remained an incredibly easy person to please. She'd complimented his cheese spread and crackers he set out for the parade, raved over the show and sighed over the table Ricky and Molly had already set when he called them to dinner—paper plates and all.

He couldn't have asked the afternoon to pass more gently. Although he couldn't convince Marina to let the kids do their part in clearing the table, or in drying and putting away the rest of the dishes, he couldn't deny he quickly grew spoiled with having her company. She made any chore easier.

"I have a confession to make," she told him, when the children snuck off to watch TV again.

"Go ahead."

"This is easier than I thought it would be."

"Helping out in the kitchen?" he asked, pretending not to understand. He needed a moment to fight down a rush of panic in case she asked for too much again.

"No, being in your home. The home you shared with another woman."

"I'm glad. After I invited you, I wondered."

"I feel sad for her—and you and the children, of course."

"We're doing all right."

"I can see that. That's why I think I'm getting used to the idea about...well, about what you said."

He stopped scouring dried potato from the bottom of a pot. "You mean about us?"

"Yes. This is better." She tilted her head and her expression became thoughtful. "I think I began realizing that after Jeremy called me the other day."

The mention of Cameron delivered a blow to Read's midsection. He turned aside his head to cough into his sleeve. "Excuse me. Tickle in my throat. I always get it this time of year because of the dry furnace heat." The explanation sounded foolish, even to him. "Um...so Cameron called?"

"To talk to me again about the documentary. At first I was going to say no, but a few days before Dean Wyman telephoned from the college where my father sometimes lectured. He told me how much the film would mean to their music department."

"So you changed your mind?"

"Not completely. But I did tell Jeremy that he could bring his aunt out to visit me next week. I know he'll use the opportunity to try to press his point." She was silent for a moment. "Do you think he's a man who knows his business?"

He damn well knew *what* he wanted, Read thought darkly, and that was Marina herself. A blind man could have seen it that day the young Brahmin had visited her. But he couldn't tell her that without exposing his true feelings.

"Who am I to judge?" he asked her instead. "He looks to be. He talks it." He shrugged, wishing she wouldn't ask him to give an opinion.

"I value your opinion, Read."

So much for staying out of it. "I'm flattered. I just don't... Sure. I have a hunch he's a powerhouse."

"Dad?"

Read glanced over his shoulder to see Ricky standing in the kitchen doorway. He looked cute with his new T-shirt over his other shirt, but there was something about the militant thrust of his son's chin that had him frowning. "What's up, bud?"

"Could I talk to you for a second?"

He lifted an eyebrow, curious about what his son wanted that couldn't be said in front of Marina. "Okay." Wiping his hands, he excused himself and followed the boy into the hallway. That didn't appear good enough for Ricky, who signaled his sister being within earshot and beckoned him into the washroom. Read really got amused when the kid even shut the door. "Hey, this must be serious."

"It is." His son folded his arms across his skinny chest and glared at him. "Just what are you doing, Dad?"

"About what?"

"With Marina? I heard what you said. Why are you throwing her at that guy?"

He couldn't have been more stunned if his son had told him he'd enlisted in the Marines. "I didn't—"

"You *did*. I came to the kitchen to ask when we were gonna have dessert and I heard you. You're going to let her go out with some other guy, and then she'll get married, and we'll never see her again."

Even as Ricky spoke, the possibility was a picture in Read's mind, but he blocked it out to try to soothe his son's pain. It was obvious the kid wasn't pleased with the prospect. "First of all, you really shouldn't have been eavesdropping. Second, Marina has every right to see whomever she wants."

"She's *ours*. We found her. You never would have. And we were the ones to tell her about you. *We* want her for our mom!"

Read didn't know why he was surprised. Hadn't they done everything but have announcements printed? "It's not that simple, Rick. Marina is... different than us."

His son frowned. "No, she isn't. She's been doing all the stuff we have. She likes us."

"She loves you. And she cares for me. But... she's special." Heaven help him, he couldn't have this conversation. "Why don't we talk about this later when we have more time?"

"Now, Dad."

"Young man, we have a guest."

"Fine. I'll ask her to marry us, myself."

"No, that's one thing you can't do." Drawing in a deep breath, Read crouched to be at eye level with the boy. "Marina's had a different life than most people, Ricky."

"I don't care if she's not American. Molly doesn't, either."

"She is American. She's what they call a first-generation American. That's like the children of the early settlers. And in many ways Marina's life has been similar to those children's in that it's been difficult at times."

Ricky frowned. "Dad, she's rich. She can buy anything she wants whenever she wants."

"Money isn't at the heart of this, and I hope you haven't tried to befriend Marina because you think you might get something out of it."

"Not me!"

"Good." The truth was that finances were an important part of this issue, but his boy didn't need to know his old man had just too much pride for his own good. "What is important here is life. Living. Being overprotected to the point that when you gain your independence, you're vulnerable to making mistakes like settling for something that isn't really right for you."

"But, Dad—"

"No, son. Trust me about this. I care for Marina too much to let her jump into something she knows nothing about. A marriage is a challenge all by itself without adding children into the scenario. Marina deserves—"

The unintended inference behind his words struck him too late.

Ricky paled and took a step back. "It's because of us?"

"I didn't mean—"

"You did! And you're a liar!"

Chapter Nine

Marina not only heard Ricky's shout, she saw him burst from the room and storm upstairs. A moment later Read brought up the rear. By then she'd reached the kitchen doorway.

"What on earth? Read, what he said..."

"It's my fault."

Molly rushed to them. "What's wrong, Daddy?"

"Nothing serious, sugarplum. Go back and watch your TV."

"But Daddy, I saw Ricky crying when he ran upstairs."

"He'll be fine. I'll go talk to him in a minute."

He should have picked her up. He should have kissed her and soothed her. Instead he raked his hands through his hair and retreated into the kitchen.

Marina took one look at Molly's puckering lower lip and stooped to embrace her. "Baby, it's all right. Why don't you do as your daddy said, and I'll find out what's wrong."

With a mournful backward look, the child went. Marina stood by and watched until she saw that Molly had settled on the couch again.

In the kitchen, she discovered that Read had resumed washing the pots and silverware from their dinner. She wasted no time getting to the point.

"I thought you were going up?"

"In a while."

But his tone suggested otherwise, and there was a stubborn set to his chin that she'd seen duplicated on Ricky's. The message she was getting from all that was too disturbing. And what she hadn't told him yet was that she had heard something.

"He called you a liar. That's hardly nothing."

Read looked shocked at first, then dismayed. But too soon his resolute mask fell back in place. "He misunderstood things, that's all."

"What things?"

Read dropped the scrubber and gripped the edge of the sink. "You, all right? You and me and . . . us."

"Oh, no." She glanced toward the stairs. Poor child. She could only imagine what Ricky had hoped—the same as she had. But she wanted to be certain. "If what you discussed includes me, don't I have a right to know the details?"

"No. Let him have a few minutes to get used to the idea."

"What idea?"

He exhaled sharply, the sound sheer exasperation. "That things don't always work out the way you want them to. Look, Marina, he and Molly are beginning to think that you were going to take Gwenn's place. Don't tell me that after that day in town when they were taking that video, and asking all those questions, you didn't realize what they had in mind? If not then, then all these weeks when they've been begging and wheedling to spend every spare minute they could with you?"

She did on one level. On another she'd just wanted to give two beautiful children the loving attention all children deserved.

"Read, this is terrible."

"Tell me about it."

"Let me go up to him?"

"No. Things are bad enough as it is."

"That's an awful thing to say."

Suddenly Read spun around and whispered harshly, "It isn't when he already thinks that you're like some treasure he found on a bank of a creek or in some forgotten pocket. Finders keepers. Bingo, he and Molly have a new mommy." He closed his eyes and shook his head. "I just wish I didn't say what I did. The words came out all wrong, and now he thinks . . ."

"What does he think?"

"I tried to explain to him that not everyone thinks a ready-made family is an asset."

"You didn't. How could you? Today of all days!" She flung down the towel she'd just reached for and started toward the stairs.

Read grabbed her. "Where are you going?"

"To talk to him."

"Absolutely not. Haven't you been listening? You'll only make things worse."

"You've told him something that would be difficult for an older child to comprehend, Read. He's only a little boy!"

But Read's grip grew tighter instead of easing. "He's *my* son, Marina."

He might as well have told her to stay out of his business. The message went straight to her heart and lodged there like a dagger. Staring at the resolute message in his eyes, she shook her head.

"Shame on you, Read. I was childish to try to use Jeremy Cameron to see if I could make you jealous. But I see what you're doing, and that's worse than wrong. It's despicable. If you want to keep a barrier between us, that's your right. But shame on you for using your children as insurance, in case your resolve weakens."

She wrenched her arm free and walked out of the room. She went straight to Molly and hugged her. "Angel? I have to go."

The child immediately wrapped her arms around her neck. "No! Why?"

"I'll explain sometime soon. In the meantime I want you to promise me something. Be sure to tell Ricky that I love him. I love you both, and I want you to know that you're still welcome at The Christmas House anytime, okay?"

"I don't understand. Marina? Marina!"

"Bye, baby."

"Marina!"

She jerked at the sharp sound of her name and saw Mrs. Cotton scowling at her. "Excuse me?"

"What do you mean you won't try these?"

Had she said that? She glanced at the checkbook she'd been working on balancing, then at Mrs. Cotton's round concerned face. In the old woman's hand was a tin box of fudge. "Oh. I didn't realize..."

"I made it myself last night after I got home. I thought about how your treats have caught on so well, and how you've been staying up all hours making them, and the least I could do is give you one evening's rest."

"Why, Mrs. Cotton, how very kind of you." Unfortunately, she had no appetite whatsoever, hadn't had one in days. But not wanting to risk hurting the old woman's feelings twice, she forced herself to take one of the bite-size pieces of candy rolled in crushed nuts. "They look delicious."

"Emily's going to make her famous no-bake fruitcake tonight, so don't you worry about trying to make anything tonight, either. You're getting so pale lately, we're beginning to worry about you."

"I'm fine, really."

"Em just has to stop at the market on the way home and pick up the candied cherries," Mrs. Cotton continued as if she hadn't spoken. "She called me last night and said it was the only thing she lacked. Asked did I think it was all right if she left them out. I told her, 'Em, have you been seasoning everything with rum again? A fruitcake isn't a fruitcake without the cherries!'"

"My goodness, neither of you should be going through so much trouble. This is my responsibility." Touched but concerned, because both Mrs. Cotton and Mrs. Merriweather were already working nearly a full schedule since business had picked up, Marina studied the small woman with the same intensity her employee had examined her. "In fact, I've been going over the books and I can see we can afford to hire another clerk."

"That's wonderful, dear. The more the merrier. But don't worry about us. Why, we're having a ball. Never felt better in our lives."

"Well, I want to make sure you stay that way. Do you know of anyone in your neighborhood who's looking for some extra cash for the holidays?"

"You tell me how many bodies you need, sweetie, and I'll bring them along. Our senior-citizen Bible study group is loaded with able souls bored with being put out to pasture. Winnie Livingston strikes me as your best bet, though. She raised nine children and has seventeen grandkids as of this past July Fourth, and she knows how to deal with people of all ages."

"She sounds perfect. Do you have her phone number by any chance?"

"You just leave that to me." Mrs. Cotton set her tin of candies on the front counter. "She lives across the street from me and I've been telling her all about you. She can't wait to start."

Bemused, and glad to have her mind off her personal worries for a change, Marina shook her head. "You're quite something, Mrs. Cotton."

"I know it, dear. But I look at it this way, why waste time being something you're not? I fought being myself for forty years trying to please Mr. Cotton, only there was no pleasing that old stick-in-the-mud. Now that I'm on my own, I'm letting it all hang out."

As the silver-haired elf waved and went off to help prepare the rooms for another day's business, Marina looked from her to the candy she had yet to taste, and realized she had more in common with Ruby Cotton than she could have guessed. She was asserting herself, too—only she was being far less successful at it than her new friend.

At least business was no longer a worry. Read had been right about things turning around after Thanksgiving. At least she could give him that.

In the week since she'd seen him, they hadn't spoken. Before her was an updated statement of what he'd built for her, and what he still owed her, along with an estimated schedule as to when he would complete each piece. It had come in the mail yesterday. Considering the way they'd parted on Thanksgiving, she wondered if he would freight her furniture over, as well.

A familiar ache resumed its dull wrenching in her chest. She'd had a brief reprieve from it for a few weeks, but now it was back with a vengeance. She was fast coming to the conclusion that love was meant for a stronger sort than she.

The mere thought of what he was doing to them, all of them, hurt. She missed Molly and Ricky terribly, and she doubted they understood. She lived for the day she would have a chance to explain that it changed nothing about how she felt about them.

About to go back to finishing writing a check, she was interrupted by the ringing telephone. "The Christmas House," she said into the receiver.

"Marina? Jeremy here. How's Berryfield's most beautiful businesswoman?"

"When I see her, I'll ask on your behalf."

He murmured a low, sexy growl. "Wrong answer, dear heart. What's the matter, having a bad day?"

There was an understatement. "I'm fine. How are you, Jeremy?"

"Couldn't be better now that it's only twenty-four hours before I see you again."

Marina's gaze flew to her calendar and she sighed inwardly. She liked Jeremy, his intellect and unapologetic flirtatiousness, but she'd developed a sixth sense for recognizing people intent on control, and wanted as little to do with them as possible. "To be perfectly honest, Jeremy, I'd forgotten. We've been very busy since Friday, and I've completely lost track of time."

He was silent for a moment, as if weighing his options. "What are you telling me? Do you need to postpone tomorrow, or are we talking about a full withdrawal?"

Lord, the man worked fast. One meeting and he made them sound as if they had the most complicated of relationships. Didn't he realize that two in one lifetime was more than enough for anyone?

"Well, let me change my approach," he said, almost cheerfully. "Has Vladimir called you lately?"

She had to think fast to keep up with him. "Um... no, not in a few days." Not since lecturing her for not agreeing on the spot to accept Jeremy's proposal.

"Then let me be the first to congratulate you. He's arranged for your father's complete works to be released as a special CD collection."

"That's... wonderful."

"It's perfect. Between the collection and the documentary, we'll have the media covered for weeks."

"Jeremy—"

"Do you know who I want to direct the film? Marge Thornton, who you'll remember just won an Oscar this year. She's an old school chum, who also happens to be a great devotee of your father's work."

"Jeremy..."

"You're letting yourself get frightened off by the idea that we're talking about a probing interview. That's not what I want from you. You open the program—in front of his piano, perhaps. I see you in a formal gown...black velvet, cut off those glorious shoulders. The camera will adore you. You say a few words, something anecdotal, and that's it as far as on-camera work for you until midway through. It's all off-screen narration until then. Halfway through you're back on-screen in another part of the house, or out in that garden beyond his room—or maybe we'll get the college to let us use one of his old class-rooms—then more narration. At the end you stand on the stage at Lincoln Center and look out at the empty seats that he used to fill. You say something about his voice being silent now, but his music will live on forever. Walk offstage and credits roll. Like it?"

She felt as if the room was closing in on her. "You have been giving this considerable thought."

"Believe it. I'm not one to let opportunity slip by me, lovely lady."

"You will this time, Jeremy," she said politely but firmly. "I'm afraid I'm exhausted. I'm already short-handed here, and if I have any free time, I'm going to need it to meet with craftsmen to continue stocking my store. I'm sorry, but that's the way I feel."

"You won't get rid of me that easily. I see star potential written all over you, Marina, and I don't intend to let you slip through my fingers."

But she didn't want to be a star. She wanted her own life . . . and to live it with the man she loved.

As if she'd conjured him from her imagination, she looked up and saw him standing in the foyer doorway.

He must have come in the back way, and either Mrs. Cotton or Mrs. Merriweather must have let him in. He looked as uncomfortable as she suddenly felt.

"Marina? Did you go to sleep on me?"

"No, I'm here, Jeremy. But someone's come in and I do need to go."

She should have taken pleasure in seeing what saying Jeremy's name did to Read's already grim face. But as she said goodbye and hung up, all she felt was another wrenching inside, and an awareness that her hands had begun to tremble.

"I'm sorry for interrupting."

"You didn't."

He looked wonderful. Tired, and as if he wasn't eating any more than she was, but wonderful anyway. He was wearing work clothes, his rugged denim jacket and dusty, rumpled jeans, and he carried the smell of man and wood about him. It reminded her of how safe and feminine a woman felt in his solid and strong arms.

"I only wanted you to know I've brought the unit for the stuffed animals. But maybe you better look at it before I leave. It wasn't what we'd discussed and you may not want it."

She didn't want to deal with this. She didn't think she had the strength left to pretend she was fine and that life was going on beautifully without him. But what he'd said could mean trouble, and if he had changed the design so that the piece didn't suit her needs, she would rather he take it back now, instead of having to call him back for yet another visit.

Pushing away from her desk and the piece of fudge that remained untouched, she rose and quickly buried her hands deep into the pockets of her lacy white apron which, like Mrs. Cotton and Mrs. Merriweather, she wore over a Victorian white blouse and floor-length Christmas-plaid skirt.

She felt Read's gaze like a physical touch as she approached him. Even though she kept her eyes lowered, her awareness of him brought a familiar heat to her cheeks. She hated her body's betrayal, just as she resented his power over her.

"You look like you stepped out of a fairy tale."

His words were a rough whisper and sounded reluctant. Out of necessity she ignored them. "Where did you put it?"

After a slight hesitation, he replied more heavily, "In the living room. But I think when you have the dining room ready, you might want to put it in there. It needs more room."

Without further comment, she headed for that room. Both Mrs. Cotton and Mrs. Merriweather were there, turning on lights and adjusting displays. When they spotted her and Read, Mrs. Cotton clasped her hands under her double chin.

"Oh, Mr. Archer, the train is the sweetest thing. The children are going to want to climb right in with these cute bears."

Only as she rounded the couch did Marina see what she was talking about. Instead of the oversize treasure chest she'd asked for, he'd created a three-car oversize wooden train. The engine was a bright red with a wonderful brass bell behind its steam stack, the next car a bright yellow, the next a vibrant blue and the last a shiny green.

"And look how the wheels turn," Mrs. Merriweather said, bending at the waist like a giraffe reaching for water to roll it back and forth. "Have you ever seen anything like it?"

Marina didn't have the heart to deny Read the praise he deserved. "It's delightful, Read. Thank you."

"Are you sure? I didn't think about the kids wanting to pull it through the whole house."

"But a house doesn't become a real home unless it's lived in," she said, remembering having heard that somewhere. She managed a wry smile for him. "However, I have a hunch we're going to get a considerable number of requests from parents for the train itself. You may find yourself with more work than you can handle."

"That's all right. I've discovered I have a great deal of free time these days."

Between the sad timbre in his voice and the compelling power of his gaze, Marina knew he'd intrigued both of her keen-sensed employees. To escape their sharp inspection, she gestured for him to follow her to her desk.

"In that case, if you'll give me the statement, I'll write you a check right away."

"I didn't mean that in the way you took it, and I didn't bring a bill. Molly knocked over a can of varnish on my entire box of invoice forms. I have to go reorder more after I leave here."

The mention of the child created a lump in her throat. She had to ask, "How is she?"

"Let me put it this way, the spill is the most recent so-called mishap to get my attention. In the meantime Ricky stays in his room and refuses to come out except to go to school."

Was he blaming her? Did he think she could help? "I don't know what to say."

"There's nothing to say. I brought this on myself. I'll figure out how to undo the pain I caused. I did want to..."

Marina looked up when his words drifted into silence. "Yes?"

"I wish things could have been different."

Weary with words, she shook her head. "I'm not sure whether it's a matter of not believing you, or that I just don't care anymore. In any case, go home, Read. We don't have anything left to say to one another."

Read spent the rest of the day in a state of deep depression, followed by another and another. A week slipped into two, then three.

There came a point when if he hadn't had his kids to worry about, he knew he would have been at the nearest bar drowning his sorrow in beer. But he was a single parent, and reckless behavior was a luxury he couldn't afford.

Instead he spent hour after hour, day after day in his workshop, more often than not staring at the floor. The gray slab of concrete aptly resembled the state of his life. Most of the time, he sat and replayed Marina's last words in his mind.

She hated him. Somehow his good intentions had gone awry, causing his efforts to fall into a black hole with them. All he could think of now was that she despised him for what he'd become. What he'd tried to do meant nothing.

He was sitting one afternoon when Ricky and Molly arrived from school. He saw his son go straight into the house without even looking at him. His daughter approached more readily, but still without the zest and love she used to.

When she was close he opened his arms. "Can I have a hug? I need one bad today."

She complied and even added a noisy kiss on his cheek. It made him feel very lucky.

"I made a picture of Marina and us at The Christmas House today." She held it up before his face, almost hitting him in the nose with it. "Can we go see her so I can take it to her?"

Read groaned inwardly. "No, honey. I'm afraid not."

"But Ricky could walk me if you said yes, Daddy. He's good with streets."

"It's not the streets, sugarplum."

"Then what now? It's been forever."

"Marina needs some time alone. She's very busy and—"

"Did you make her mad at you again?"

Ricky's sharp voice jarred him. He looked over Molly's curls to see him standing in the doorway, his hands balled into small fists.

"Son, I know I said that in a few weeks maybe you could go see her, but things haven't worked out the way I'd—"

"You did! You ruined things. You always do!"

He charged from the shop despite Read's call for him to stop. Beside him Molly stood by and eyed him sadly. After several seconds he met her sorrowful gaze and sighed.

"Go ahead. Say it."

"What are we gonna do, Daddy?"

"Go on. We've been fine up until now, haven't we?"

She shook her head. "We don't do so good alone, Daddy. Ricky has to take care of me, 'cause you're out here all the time, and there's nobody to take care of you. We're getting confused, Daddy."

Her soft voice brought the accuracy of their situation home with razor-blade precision, and Read hugged her more tightly. "Ah, sweetheart, I'm sorry. I'm sorry."

"I just don't understand. Why can't Marina be our new mommy?" she whimpered.

"It's grown-up stuff, baby. Hard to explain."

"Did I do something wrong?"

He groaned and pressed a kiss to her smooth forehead. "No, sweet. You're as close to perfect as a little girl can get."

"Well, if Ricky didn't do nothin' and I didn't do nothin', what happened? I love Marina, Daddy. Is she going away like Mommy went away?"

Read swallowed hard. "*No*. Don't even think that. Marina would never leave you, baby. As for the rest, you have to give me some time to think, because I just don't have the answers right now."

"Well, who do you talk to to get answers, Daddy? Santa?"

"Yeah, maybe Santa, babe."

Chapter Ten

"Marina, dear, why don't you come with us?" Mrs. Cotton said, lifting her crocheted shawl over her silver bun. She eyed her broodingly as she wound the long, fringe-tipped wrap around and around her neck. "I hate to think of you here all by yourself on Christmas Eve."

"I won't be alone all night," Marina replied, securing a missed button on the old woman's coat. "I'm planning to go to a candlelight service later, remember?"

"Alone," Mrs. Merriweather grumbled, tugging on knit gloves.

"Go to our church with us," Winnie Livingston pleaded, looking up from the boots she was tugging on. In the chandelier light the newest employee's hair matched her pastel blue glasses. "It's mostly half-deaf old people so we sing off-key, but we do have a good time.''

Marina managed to smile, grateful for the invitation as she was for the friendship they'd established these past weeks. But she shook her head. ''I love that you asked me, ladies. And I promise I will think about your invitation for dinner tomorrow. But I think I'm going to turn in rather early tonight.''

It had been a busy day. Because it was Christmas Eve, shoppers had begun arriving the moment Marina had opened the front gates, and the last one had left only minutes ago. It was now almost five o'clock, and Marina was sending her employees home before it grew completely dark outside.

The Christmas House had achieved a successful first season of business. Three months ago this had only been a dream, and they had far to go and a number of adjustments and improvements to make. But despite that, and the heartache, she had good memories, and she wanted to be alone for a while to reflect on them as she went from room to room, turning off all the lights.

Hugging each woman again, she gently coaxed them out the front door and waved as they drove away. When she saw them turning out onto the street, she sighed, retreated into the house and locked the door behind her.

Her mouth ached from smiling; her head ached from making small talk all day. She appreciated the group's concern for her, but she was glad they'd gone home to prepare for their neighborhood gathering that would follow church services. She wanted to be alone, to be with her own thoughts, dwelling on those closest to her heart.

It had been weeks since she'd seen Read. Days since she'd seen the children. On impulse she'd done some shopping and had gifts for them up in her room, but now she didn't know what to do about them. She'd hoped that they would have come over this week, and she would have presented them then, but that hadn't happened. If she called the house, would Read let her drop them off on her way to the church service? Maybe they weren't even home....

For the next two hours she went through the house double-checking that all the doors were secured, the tree lights and display lights off. Satisfied, she went upstairs and took a long, luxurious bath using some of the contents from the freesia-scented gift basket her new friends had given her. Afterward, she used the matching scented lotion on her skin.

The dress she'd set out on her bed was a black velvet sheath, not nearly as daring as the one Jeremy had described. It reminded her that she had another message from him on her desk. He'd called almost every two or three days to press her about the film, or ask her out—or both. Once the holidays were over and she had more time on her hands, she would have to address the matter of the film. She was beginning to believe she was ready to help give the world its image of the Dmitri Davidov it wanted without feeling like an impostor herself.

As for Jeremy...well, Jeremy was Jeremy. Few women would find him easy to deal with, and she knew now that fate hadn't meant her to try, beyond friendship. She and his aunt had finally met, and she chuckled softly as she remembered how they'd come to that same conclusion. Maybe together they would find the right woman for him. "Get our revenge," Bianca Cameron had whispered conspiratorially.

She stepped into the simple but elegant dress and slipped into the black high heels with the pretty faux-pearl buttons on the front. Adding a choker pearl necklace and studs in her ears, she picked up her evening coat, leather gloves and bag and hesitated by the gifts. There were too many to carry in one trip, not with her coat and things. She started downstairs, thinking she would put her things at the door, get a large shopping bag and—

At the bottom she thought she saw a flash of lights in the window, but she decided it had been a car on the street. About to head for the kitchen where she kept the bags, she backtracked to the phone. She would call Read. Nervous or not, the sooner she got the call behind her, the sooner she would know what to do with the presents.

But when she rang the house there was no answer. She couldn't imagine where they could be, unless he'd treated them to dinner out before taking them to church, too. Her heart beat faster at the thought of seeing them there. Read. Would he acknowledge her or pretend he didn't see her?

A sound caught her attention. It was singing. Carolers?

Delighted, she went to the door and smiled at the sight of two flashlights illuminating two youthful faces, rosy pink from the cold and snow flurries that had begun to fall again. But when she recognized the faces, she gasped.

"On the fourth day of Christmas," they began to sing.

Ricky and Molly? She couldn't believe it! As she pressed her hand to her mouth to hold back a tremulous laugh, they sang through the chorus.

But where was Read? Surely the little imps hadn't slipped from the house on their own without telling him?

As she searched the well-lit grounds for a sign of him, the children began, "On the fifth day of Christmas, my true love gave to me—"

The rest of the stanza was lost to her because at that moment she saw a movement. Barely fighting back a small scream, she saw Read step out from the corner...Read holding out a blue box to her. A small velvet box.

Marina stared at it, then at him. "I don't understand," she murmured, as he stopped before her.

"It's not five of them like the song says," he began, carefully opening the lid. "But if it's the right kind, maybe one ring will do?"

The wall fixture lights picked up the brilliant flash of the solitaire diamond in the slender-banded engagement ring. Its brightness burned Marina's eyes and raised goose bumps all over her body.

"Oh, Read."

"Marina Davidov, will you do me the honor of becoming my wife?"

Could this be a dream? As if in slow motion, she saw him take the ring out of the box and slip the box into his pocket.

"Don't tell me you've forgotten your line?" he asked, as the children rushed closer to watch.

"No, I— I don't understand." But she automatically held out her left hand as he reached for it. Nor did she pull back when he slipped on the ring. "You said—"

"Forget what I said. The truth is that I've stopped running away from the truth. I can't bear the thought of living the rest of my life without you. I love you, Marina. Be my wife?" he asked a little less confidently.

Did he think she needed to think about it? "Yes, yes, yes!" she cried, wrapping her arms around his neck.

He kissed her then, while the children shouted into the night and hopped up and down in glee. Within seconds, she forgot the night's cold bite. If she had Read's strong arms around her, she knew she would never feel cold again.

Suddenly she felt another, smaller pair of arms wrap around her waist. Then another around her hips.

"Hey, don't forget me!" Ricky demanded.

"Me, too!" Molly said, rubbing her cheek against Marina's soft skirt.

Laughing, Read released Marina, and she drew the children inside. While Read shut the door, she hugged and kissed Ricky, and then picked up Molly to do it all again.

"Why do I have a feeling that you two were in on this?" she asked them.

"Because we were!" Ricky announced proudly.

Molly nodded, her curls bouncing every which way. "Yeah, we keeped the secret good, huh?"

"Wonderfully good," Marina said, her heart brimming with love. "So good you two merry matchmakers deserve a surprise. Why don't you run upstairs to my room. I think Santa left some early presents for you on my bed.''

No sooner did she set Molly down than the two of them charged for the stairs, whooping with excitement. Marina watched them for a few seconds before feeling Read take hold of her arms.

"How long do you think we have before they charge down here again?" he murmured, drawing her close.

Once again her body tingled with pleasure. "A few minutes. I was very bad and spoiled them a great deal."

"Remind me to punish you later, but right now that sounds like heaven. Let's not waste a second," he replied, and locked his mouth to hers.

Now came the kiss she'd been longing for, dreaming of. It soothed the weeks of grief and loneliness, and promised the fulfillment of the passion that had always simmered between them whenever they touched. By the time Read lifted his head to catch his breath, she was clinging to him to keep from melting to the floor.

"Read," she whispered, unable to keep from brushing her lips against his again and again. "I can't believe this."

"Believe it. I couldn't go on the way things were." He stroked his cheek against hers. "Being a proud and stubborn fool made me miserable and nearly cost me my kids. I not only broke your heart, darling, I broke theirs, too.

"I'm sorry for being prejudiced against your father's success," he continued, straightening to gaze deep into her eyes. "I'm sorry for one minute throwing you at someone else, and then being a jealous fool in the next. I want you to know that I'll try to support whatever you do in honor of your father's memory. I may not be the greatest fan of his kind of music, but I happen to be nuts about his greatest composition."

After he kissed her again, Marina touched his cheek. "I am going to tell Jeremy Cameron that I'll do the documentary, Read. It's time, and I think it will do a lot to free me from the past."

Although he nodded readily, a gleam also entered his eye. "But would you at least hold off until after the wedding? I don't trust that shark around you."

"You have nothing to fear from Jeremy, Read," Marina murmured, stroking his cheek with the backs of her fingers. "It's you I want."

Read's arms tightened around her. "Sweetheart..."

His next kiss unraveled some of the finer threads of their control. Their hands became more restless, seeking and coaxing; their bodies inched closer and closer, desperately trying to assuage the yearning that strained to be fulfilled.

At last Read buried his face against her throat and crushed her close to hold her still. "I want you," he groaned. "I want you so much."

"I want you, too."

They both sighed and exchanged wry smiles as the sound of small feet on the stairs stopped them from saying anything more. They glanced up to see Ricky and Molly descending with their favorite gifts tucked under their arms.

"Dad, look! Marina gave me a microscope and there's a neat science kit upstairs, too!" Ricky declared, his eyes sparkling.

"And I got this angel doll, Daddy. Isn't she beautiful? She has hair just like mine, and I got a comb-and-brush set like Marina's and jewelry!"

As Read lifted an eyebrow at her, Marina went down on her knees to accept the hugs and kisses from each child. "I'm so glad you like your presents."

"We do," Ricky assured her. "But the best of all is that you and Dad are gonna get married. Does that mean we'll get to live here with you?"

Although her heart leaped in joy, Marina forced herself to say quietly, "We'll have to see what your dad says about that."

He looked from one expectant pair of eyes to another. "Why do I get the feeling that I'm woefully outnumbered?"

They were married on New Year's Eve. When people teased them about the short engagement, Read told them about how he'd suggested they catch a late flight to Las Vegas on Christmas Eve.

Molly was Marina's maid of honor and Ricky walked her down the aisle of the small chapel at the center of town and then stood up as Read's best man. Read invited the Fields family and Marina's guests were her new circle of friends from The Christmas House, who all wept profusely and afterward told her that it was the most romantic ceremony they'd ever witnessed. Jeremy politely declined the invitation to attend, but sent a case of champagne for the reception.

They held the brief reception at The Christmas House, but it wasn't long before Mrs. Cotton took control by handing everyone their coats. She even insisted on having Ricky and Molly spend the night with her.

"Mrs. Merriweather will make her famous caramel popcorn," she told them. "Mrs. Livingston's made brownies that will melt in your mouth, and we've rented a half-dozen Cary Grant movies from the video store."

"Who's Cary Grant?" they heard Molly whisper to Ricky, as the three ladies ushered him and Molly out the front door.

Finally alone, Read turned to Marina. The laughter that had lit his eyes only moments before was quickly replaced with something far more profound and intimate. When he stretched out his hand, Marina went to him eagerly.

"Now...? Or do you need a few minutes?" he asked, stroking her hair.

She smiled. "Now. I've had ten years to get ready for you."

Leaving Raspberry, who slept comfortably before the living room fireplace, they crossed the foyer. About to set her foot on the first stair, Marina felt herself swept off her feet and into Read's arms.

"I don't get to carry you over the threshold," he said, holding her close to his heart, "so if you don't mind..."

How could she possibly have minded? Since Christmas Eve, he was continually doing and saying things that either thrilled her or filled her eyes with tears of heartfelt emotion. Telling him so, she wrapped her arms around his neck and offered him the kiss of promise.

In her bedroom—their bedroom now, because he'd already moved many of his things here—he set her on her feet, and for a moment simply gazed at her with wonder and very male possessiveness.

"You're so beautiful."

She was glad he liked the wisteria blue silk gown she'd chosen to be wed in. But she believed that he was responsible for any real beauty that he saw in her. "Make love to me, Read. I ache for you so."

"Marina. I'll be loving you until I take my last breath."

And as he framed her face with his hands and kissed her deeply, Read showed her how well he intended to keep his promise.

*   *   *   *   *   *

COMING NEXT MONTH

#1126 A FATHER'S VOW—Elizabeth August
Fabulous Fathers/Smytheshire, Massachusetts
When Lucas Carver's little boy picked the lovely Felicity Burrow as his mother, Lucas knew she was perfect. For Felicity touched his heart and mind in ways neither of them had dreamed possible.

#1127 THE BABY FACTOR—Carolyn Zane
Bundles of Joy
Elaine Lewis *would* keep custody of her baby—even if it meant a temporary marriage to her employee Brent Clark. But leaning on Brent's loving strength soon had this independent lady thinking of a ready-made family!

#1128 SHANE'S BRIDE—Karen Rose Smith
Hope Franklin left Shane Walker years ago to avoid tying him down with a child. But now Hope knew their son needed a father, and she owed Shane the truth....

**#1129 THE MAVERICK TAKES A WIFE—
Charlotte Moore**
Logan Spurwood had enough problems without falling for Marilee Haggerty. He had nothing to offer her; his past had made sure of that. But Logan couldn't stay away or stop dreaming of a happy future with Marilee.

#1130 THE MARRIAGE CHASE—Natalie Patrick
When heiress Felicia Grantham decided on a convenient marriage, no one could stop her—not even dashing Ethan Bradshaw. But Ethan's bold manner took her breath away, and soon Felicia was determined to follow her plan—with Ethan as the groom!

#1131 HIS SECRET SON—Betty Jane Sanders
Amy Sutherland traveled to the wilderness to find Matt Gray. He certainly wasn't the man she'd imagined as her nephew's father, but she hoped to persuade this rugged loner to accept the boy she loved.

MILLION DOLLAR SWEEPSTAKES (III)

It's our 1000th Special Edition and we're celebrating!

Join us these coming months for some wonderful stories in a special celebration of our 1000th book with some of your favorite authors!

Diana Palmer   **Nora Roberts**
Debbie Macomber   **Christine Flynn**
Phyllis Halldorson   **Lisa Jackson**

Plus miniseries by:

Lindsay McKenna, Marie Ferrarella, Sherryl Woods and Gina Ferris Wilkins.

And many more books by special writers!

And as a special bonus, all Silhouette Special Edition titles published during Celebration 1000! will have **_double_** Pages & Privileges proofs of purchase!

Silhouette Special Edition...heartwarming stories packed with emotion, just for you! You'll fall in love with our next 1000 special stories!

1000BK-R

SOMETIMES BIG SURPRISES
COME IN SMALL PACKAGES!

THE BABY FACTOR
Carolyn Zane

Single mom Elaine Lewis would do anything to keep her baby—even marry her employee Brent Clark! Of course, they'd only planned on a temporary marriage. But Brent made a great groom and a wonderful dad, and soon this independent lady was having dreams of a *real* family!

Coming in January from

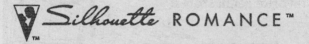

BOJ5

You're About to Become a

Privileged Woman

Reap the rewards of fabulous free gifts and benefits with proofs-of-purchase from Silhouette and Harlequin books

Pages & Privileges™

It's our way of thanking you for buying our books at your favorite retail stores.

PROOF OF PURCHASE
SR-PP88
Offer expires October 31, 1996

Pages & Privileges ™

**Harlequin and Silhouette—
the most privileged readers in the world!**

For more information about Harlequin and Silhouette's PAGES & PRIVILEGES program call the Pages & Privileges Benefits Desk: 1-503-794-2499